FAVOR

A Novel by

Parnell Hall

AN ONYX BOOK

NEW AMERICAN LIBRARY

A DIVISION OF PENGUIN BOOKS USA INC.

PUBLISHER'S NOTE

This book is a work of fiction. Names, characters, places, and incidents either are the product of the author's imagination or are used fictitiously, and any resemblance to actual persons, living or dead, events, or locales is entirely coincidental.

Copyright © 1988 by Parnell Hall

This is an authorized reprint of a hardcover edition published by Donald I. Fine, Inc. The hardcover edition was published in Canada by General Publishing Company Limited.

 ONYX TRADEMARK REG. U.S. PAT. OFF. AND FOREIGN COUNTRIES
REGISTERED TRADEMARK—MARCA REGISTRADA
HECHO EN DRESDEN, TN, U.S.A.

SIGNET, SIGNET CLASSIC, MENTOR, ONYX, PLUME, MERIDIAN and NAL BOOKS are published by New American Library, a division of Penguin Books USA Inc., 1633 Broadway, New York, New York 10019

First Onyx Printing, November, 1989

1   2   3   4   5   6   7   8   9

PRINTED IN THE UNITED STATES OF AMERICA

FOR JIM AND FRANNY

1

"I have a daughter."

"Oh?"

There was no reason for me to be surprised. MacAullif certainly had every right to have a daughter. After all, he was somewhere around fifty, and he was a big, solid, virile-looking man, presumably capable of having produced any number of daughters. He wasn't the handsomest man in the world by any stretch of the imagination, but he wasn't the ugliest either, and it wasn't inconceivable that in his youth he had been attractive and agreeable enough to have wooed and wed a young lady and raised a family. So there was no reason for me to be surprised.

But I was.

You see, MacAullif was a cop.

I know that doesn't make any sense. That's because the fault did not lie in MacAullif, or in his being a cop, but in me. You see, my problem is my view of the world is colored by my own personal preconceptions and misconceptions. And one of my severe failings is an inability to attribute personal lives to people I meet on a professional basis. That is to say, if I'm being examined by the doctor, I tend to think of him as a doctor, and it doesn't occur to me that maybe he has a wife he wants to get home to, or perhaps *he* has a cold.

And with cops, it's ten times worse. Cops are authority figures. They're intimidating. They're the law. Somehow, you never really think of a cop as having a family. Except cops that get shot, of course. Cops who get shot inevitably have a wife and at least three kids. But the cops who pull you over and give you a ticket never have any families at all.

Now MacAullif was not only a cop, he was a homicide cop, and a sergeant to boot. I'd met him in the course of two homicide investigations. The first time had been in passing. The second time had been longer, seeing as how I'd been cast in the role of the murder suspect. So I'd gotten to know him pretty well.

But on a professional basis.

This was something else.

MacAullif took out a cigar, unwrapped it, and surveyed the end of it gloomily. I knew he wasn't going to smoke it—his doctor had made him give them up. He just liked to play with them now and then. Particularly when he had something to say.

We were sitting alone in MacAullif's office. He had called me up and asked me to come down. He hadn't said why, so I had no idea what I was doing there. At least I had no idea when I came. Now I assumed it had something to do with his daughter, unless MacAullif was just making polite conversation. Somehow I doubted it. MacAullif wasn't much of a one for small talk.

MacAullif eyed the cigar as if it were a perpetrator. "Yeah, I have a daughter," he said.

I had a sudden flash. The cigar was a phallic symbol, the perpetrator was a rapist, and his daughter'd been attacked.

I felt a wave of sympathy for MacAullif. Fortunately, I didn't express it, for, as usual, I was dead wrong.

"She's twenty-eight," MacAullif said. "Lives in a suburb of Atlantic City. She's married; she's got a daughter, seven."

Jesus. MacAullif had a daughter *and* a granddaughter.

"I see," I said. I didn't see at all.

"They were up last weekend. They stayed with us. Me and the missus. At our house. We got a house in Brooklyn. Bay Ridge."

Things were coming thick and fast. MacAullif had a house in Brooklyn. A house with a woman in it. The missus. A woman waiting to hug the old side of beef when he got home from work.

My additions to the conversation thus far had not been earth-shattering. To them I now added, "Yes."

MacAullif leaned back in his chair, took a deep breath, and blew it out again.

"My son-in-law came with them. He's thirty. Dark hair, blue eyes, five-ten, a hundred sixty pounds."

I realized what I'd just heard was a police description. I also realized MacAullif had just identified the perpetrator. The situation, such as it was, was beginning to take shape.

"His name is Harold. Harold Dunleavy," MacAullif said. He added, belatedly, "Oh, I didn't tell you my daughter's name. It's Barbara."

As he said that, I suddenly realized I didn't know MacAullif's name either. He knew my name—Stanley Hastings—but then, he'd interrogated me in a murder investigation. In such circumstances, it is standard procedure to ask the suspect's name. It is not standard procedure for the suspect to ask the interrogator's, however. So the only first name I'd ever heard MacAullif addressed by was Sergeant.

MacAullif raised his eyes and looked at the wall

behind me, another habit he had when he was thinking of what to say. I recalled from the other times I'd been in his office that the wall was covered with framed certificates. It occurred to me that his name would be on them. But I'd never noticed it, which gives you an idea of how observant I am. I didn't want to turn around and stare at them now, but I made a mental note to check his name on the way out.

MacAullif's gaze shifted to his cigar. I think he realized he was squeezing it tighter than the prescribed method for cigar holding. At any rate, he put it down. He rubbed his forehead and looked up at me.

"It's about my son-in-law," he said.

"What about him?"

MacAullif rubbed his chin. "I don't know."

"I see," I said.

MacAullif looked at me sharply, and I immediately regretted the remark. There was no way it could be considered as anything other than ironic.

"I know, I know," MacAullif said. "I don't seem to be making any sense. I'll spit it out."

He did. After his stumbling reticence, it suddenly all came pouring out.

"It's my son-in-law. There's something wrong with him. But that's not just it. There's always been something wrong with him. I never liked him, you know. I know, I know, it's natural. A father feels that way about the guy who takes away his little girl. But it's more than that. There's something wrong with him. Always has been. You gotta understand, I'm a cop. I'm a good judge of people. I know it's personal, and that makes it different. But even separating that, I can tell. And he's a wrong one, you know what I mean?"

"Yeah."

"But last weekend was different. Harold was different. He's a stockbroker, and I tell you something, if I had any stocks I sure wouldn't trust him with them. He's the type of broker, if he was on Wall Street, I'd suspect him of insider trading. I don't think they get those opportunities in Atlantic City. Where was I? Oh, yeah. He was different, somehow. I'd ask him about his work—I always did, I had to talk to him about something—and he was particularly evasive. More than usual. If I didn't know better, I would have thought he'd been fired. But if he had, Barbara would have told me. And that was the other thing. Barbara. She wasn't herself either. You know?"

I didn't know. And I felt I was knowing less and less as the conversation progressed.

"Look," I said. "Evidently your daughter and your son-in-law are having some sort of marital problems. And I'm sorry about it and I sympathize with you. But, you'll pardon me for asking, but how in the world does all this concern me?"

MacAullif sighed. A deep heavy sigh. Then he looked me right in the eye.

"I want to hire you."

2

I was shocked. Shocked and alarmed.

I have to explain. You see, I'm a private detective. But that's misleading. I'm not a *real* private detective. I'm an ambulance chaser. But that's misleading, too. What I really am is a failure.

I am a failed actor. I am also a failed writer. In between those failures, I have held a large and diverse number of temporary jobs. My current job is that of chasing ambulances for the law firm of Rosenberg & Stone. All that entails doing is interviewing the accident victims who call in in response to the firm's TV ads, taking down the facts of the case, and then photographing the scene of the accident. The thing is, doing that technically makes me a private detective, and I have a photo I.D. to prove it, which I sometimes have to do in the event someone tries to punch my face in for photographing the defect on their property that caused the client's mishap.

But the thing is, that's all I do. I don't carry a gun or do surveillance or any of that stuff private detectives do on TV. I just photograph accidents. And the only person I work for is Richard Rosenberg of Rosenberg & Stone.

In all the time I'd been a private detective, aside

from Richard Rosenberg, MacAullif was only the second person who'd ever tried to hire me. And the thing was, the first person who'd tried had wound up dead with his dick in his mouth.

I stared at MacAullif. "What?"

"I want to hire you."

"No."

"Don't be too quick to say no."

"No."

MacAullif nodded. "O.K. You've said no. Now you're under no obligation. Now hear me out."

"But—"

"Just listen."

I sighed. "O.K. Let's have it."

"Good," MacAullif said.

He got up and began pacing. His office was small and not conducive to the activity, so the fact that he tried it indicated the degree of his distress.

"The thing is, this is serious. I know it. Oh, they've had squabbles before. I'm sure the creep steps out on her now and then. It's nothing like that. It's serious. Now here's the thing. Harold's gotten into something, and whatever it is, it's bad. I mean, he's been in scrapes before, but nothing like this. This is a real humdinger. How do I know? Well, I know because I talked to him and he lied to me. I can always tell when he's lying to me, just like I can always tell when you're lying to me. But let that pass. The thing is, I'm a cop and I can tell. And whatever Harold's done this time, it's a lulu."

MacAullif paused. Considered. "Now, let's get something straight about Harold. Just in case you haven't caught my drift. Harold is a shit. A slime. A sleazeball. If the little fuck weren't married to my daughter, I'd like nothing better than to rip him apart. But he *is* married to my daughter. And that's why, if he's gotten

13

into something, I want to get him out of it. Not for his sake, you understand, but for hers."

"Why?" I blurted. I didn't mean to, it just slipped out. It was none of my business, of course. But having said it, there I was with egg on my face and MacAullif looking at me, so I said, "What I mean is, if she's so unhappy with this guy, if he's such bad news, why doesn't she just divorce him?"

"Well," MacAullif said. "For one thing, there's the kid. Betty." His face got soft. "Seven years old. Beautiful. A charmer."

"Sometimes saving a bad marriage for the sake of a kid does the kid more harm than good."

I couldn't believe I said that either. I mean, Jesus Christ, here I was talking the pros and cons of marriage and divorce with a homicide cop.

"Yeah, yeah, yeah," MacAullif said. "I heard all those arguments. Me, I'm an old-fashioned guy. I don't believe in divorce. I believe you make a commitment, you honor that commitment."

"Why? You Roman Catholic, or something?"

"No."

"Then I don't understand. You'd keep your daughter married to a creep just cause you're an old-fashioned guy?"

MacAullif shook his head irritably. "All right. All right. Maybe I overstated the case. I don't like him. But Barbara does. So he can't be all bad. Frankly, I can't see it, but give him the benefit of the doubt. Say he's just weak."

"Fine. He's just weak. So what?"

"So if he's just weak, maybe what he needs is a good kick in the teeth to get his attention. To make him sit up and take notice. Now if this scrape he's in is as bad as I think it is, maybe it's just the kind of push he needs."

I stared at MacAullif. "What you're saying is, you want your son-in-law extricated from whatever mess he's in, him and your daughter reconciled, and they all live happily ever after."

MacAullif frowned. He sat down at his desk, leaned forward, and looked at me. "What I want you to do," he said, "is go to Atlantic City, find out what's going on, let me know, and then we'll see what we can do about it."

"Why don't you hire a real detective?"

MacAullif made a face. "In the first place, I don't trust 'em. This is personal, this is private, this is not anything I want anyone to know about. In the second place, the situation doesn't call for a real detective. It calls for a gifted amateur."

I smiled. Gifted amateur was a dig. It was what MacAullif had ironically called me when we worked together on the Darryl Jackson case. "Worked together" is a loose expression. I had worked, and MacAullif had worked, and after he had run rings all around me and had enough on me to put me away, we had "worked together."

"That's very nice, but it doesn't mean anything. What do you mean, you don't trust a private detective? That's stupid."

"Oh, is it? I'm a cop. The private detectives I deal with in the course of my business usually don't happen to be on my side, you know what I mean?" He chuckled. "I could tell you stories. But the answer is no, I don't trust 'em."

"But you trust me?"

MacAullif snorted. "Yeah, I trust you." With his right index finger, he ticked off his points on the fingers of his other hand. "I trust you to hold out on me every time you get the chance. I trust you to think you're smarter than I am and to go off on your own and do your own thing. I trust you to fuck everything up at every given opportunity, and not even realize you're doing it."

"Gee, I sound like a great risk."

"You're the pits. But for all that, you wouldn't deliberately fuck me. If you'd agreed to do it, you'd look out for my interests the best you knew how."

Which was true. And I had to hand it to MacAullif. What he'd given me was probably a pretty accurate description of how he really did trust me.

Which was about how I trusted him. Except for the bit about fucking everything up. I'd learned from experience that MacAullif was usually deadly accurate.

"So what's the idea?" I said. "You want me to go down there, talk to your daughter and your son-in-law, and try to get 'em to open up and tell me what's bothering them?"

MacAullif shook his head. "Hell, no. I don't want you to meet 'em at all. Or if you did, you couldn't let 'em know who you are. You'd have to have a cover story of some kind, I don't know what. I hadn't thought about it. But I'd really rather you didn't meet 'em at all."

I stared at him. "Are you serious?"

"Absolutely. I don't want you to talk to my son-in-law. He wouldn't tell you anything. It'd be a waste of time. No. What I want you to do is put him under surveillance. Keep tabs on him and find out what he does."

I blinked. "That's your plan?"

"Yeah."

"Little skimpy, don't you think?"

MacAullif shrugged. "Hey, I don't know what's going on. Till I do, what more can I tell you?"

I shook my head. "Look. I chase ambulances. I don't do surveillance."

"Right," MacAullif said. "Just like you didn't do surveillance in the Martin Albrect case or the Darryl Jackson case."

Martin Albrect was a dead drug courier, and was also the man who had appealed to me for help and lost his genitalia. Darryl Jackson was a dead black pimp. MacAullif knew more about my involvement in those affairs than I'd have liked him to. His mentioning them was not exactly a threat, just a gentle reminder.

"I'm sorry," I said. "I can't do it."

"Why not?"

"I'm not competent."

"I think you are. I want to hire you."

"I can't let you. I'd be taking money under false pretenses. You're asking me to do something I don't think I'm qualified to do. I couldn't promise any results."

"I'm willing to take the chance."

"But I'm not. If I take your money, I'll feel obligated to you, no matter what. And then if I get in a situation where there's nothing I can do—which I think is entirely likely—I'll still feel obligated to you and feel I have to do something. Which is a no-win situation. I'll wind up having a nervous breakdown."

MacAullif sighed and rubbed his head. "This is very hard on me, you know," he said. "This is my daughter we're talking about. You got a kid, you must know how I feel. It's special." He leaned back in his chair and rubbed his head some more. "And my Barbara is some great kid, you know. I remember the day I made sergeant. Eighteen years ago. She must have been about ten. Cute, like her daughter. Anyway I made sergeant, and I wanted to celebrate, 'cause it's a big deal—not just the promotion, it's more money, the whole shmear.

"So I bought her a ten-speed bike. She'd been asking for one for months. Me, what did I know from ten speeds? For me, three speeds was a fancy bike, and damned if I ever had one. But she wanted it, and I was a sergeant, and damned if she didn't get it.

"Well, I'll never forget that afternoon. My mom was alive then, and she came over from Queens when she heard the news. And Barbara saw the taxi pull up in front of the house, and she goes tearing out the door—'Grandma, Grandma, Grandma!' And her face is all lit up like a Christmas tree, and she yells, 'Guess what!' And my mom says, 'What?' And my wife and I are standing in the front door waiting for her to tell Grandma all about the new bike she's been riding around all morning. And she turns around with this big happy smile and she points and she says, 'My daddy made sergeant!' " MacAullif shook his head. "I'll never forget it. So proud. 'My daddy made sergeant.' "

Jesus.

I must admit I don't handle sentiment well. Displays of emotion. I tend to get embarrassed. And that's just with ordinary people. People who *aren't* homicide sergeants.

The thing is, I liked MacAullif. Inasmuch as it's possible to like an adversary. And I felt sorry for him, and I felt sorry for his daughter.

But I didn't want to do it.

I shifted uncomfortably in my chair. "All right, look," I said, "I know this is very important to you. But that's just why I can't do it. It's *too* important. I can't take your money under these circumstances. Not to do something I'm not qualified to do. I'd be doing you a disservice."

MacAullif rubbed his head again. "You won't let me hire you?"

"No."

He kept rubbing his head. "I didn't think you would."

He sighed again. "All right. In that case, I have to do something I don't want to do." One more sigh, a big one this time. Then he looked up at me. "Do it as a favor."

I blinked. "What?"

"Dammit," MacAullif said, and all the helpless frustration poured out. "I'd do it myself, but I can't. They know me, for Christ's sake. I can't follow Harold around without him spotting me. Even if I could, I'm a cop, and I look like a cop. You know how welcome I'd be poking around in Atlantic City? Not to mention the fact that I happen to be up to my ass in homicides at the moment. Look, I wouldn't ask you if I weren't desperate. But I'm desperate, so I am. It's my daughter. It's personal. I need help. So I'm asking. Do it as a favor."

I didn't want to do it. But MacAullif knew the magic word. And he must have been really desperate, because he used it.

"Please."

3

I was so freaked out by what I'd agreed to do for MacAullif that I was halfway to the subway before I realized I'd neglected to check his name on the certificates on my way out.

I realize I just dated myself with the phrase *freaked out*. Yeah, I was a hippie in the sixties. Now I'm a fortyish old fogy and a disillusioned liberal. The disillusioned part has a great deal to do with not having any money. One never seems to think of that in college, however. Everything seems so grand and glorious. There you are, the cream of the cream, one of the privileged few, sipping your beer and getting a higher education. It's only later, when you get out in the real world, that the disillusionment sets in, when you realize your liberal arts degree is worth about as much as a roll of toilet paper. And has a lot fewer uses.

If college students knew what lay ahead of them, a lot more of them would study economics. Believe me, economics is the big problem. The economics of my situation, for instance, are pretty simple and pretty depressing. Working for Richard Rosenberg, I make ten bucks an hour and thirty cents a mile. If I made that every hour, I'd get four hundred a week plus expenses, which, while not princely, would be enough to get by. But it doesn't work like that. I don't get paid for an eight-hour day. I only get paid when I'm on the clock. I wear a beeper. When there's work, they beep me. When there isn't, they don't. The result is, I average somewhere between twenty and thirty hours a week, which is never quite enough.

There are two reasons why I work this draggy job. One, I can't find anything else that will pay me more than ten bucks an hour and thirty cents a mile. And two (and this is the biggie), the flexible hours were supposed to leave me time for my *real* profession: writing.

My quote, real profession, unquote, is not what one could call a steady source of income. In fact, it's not what one could call any source of income. Aside from kid's comic books and trade magazine articles, I'd never gotten anything published. Seeing as how everyone always tells me what a fabulous writer I am, this is rather depressing.

I guess I am a fairly good writer. My basic problem is I can never figure out what to write. I do know, however, that kiddies comics and trade magazine articles aren't it. When you come right down to it, given my druthers, I'd like to write *Catch-22*. The problem is, Joseph Heller has already written it. The same applies to almost anything else I'd like to write. It's too bad, 'cause I have a feeling if I could figure out what I wanted to write I'd be dangerous.

For a while I toyed with the idea of writing up my exploits in solving the Martin Albrect and Darryl Jackson cases, but I soon abandoned that. In the first place, I didn't want anyone to know about it. In the second place, those adventures, while absolutely hair-raising to me, were rather humdrum compared to your usual detective story. The average TV detective would knock off one of my little adventures in fifteen minutes flat, including commercials, leaving him forty-five minutes to sit around twiddling his thumbs until the end of the program.

That was the problem. My adventures didn't work with your typical macho hero in the role. They only worked for me. And the problem was, if I wrote it that way, if I told it like it is, as Howard Cosell would say, no publisher in the world was going to accept a manuscript where the leading character was a cowardly, incompetent, bungling fool.

Peddling the movie rights would be even worse. I could imagine the call my agent would have to make: "Manny? . . . This is Warren . . . Yeah. . . . I got a property here. Great part in it for Rob . . . Yeah. He plays a chicken-shit asshole . . . Hello? . . . Hello? . . . Manny? . . . Hello?"

No, writing up my exploits was out. And there wasn't any other writing work of any sort on the horizon. My only source of income at the moment was the pittance paid by Rosenberg & Stone. And I had just agreed to take time off from that to go to Atlantic City on a hopelessly unpromising case for which I had refused to accept a fee. And all this at a time when I was behind on the rent, behind on Con Ed, behind on the phone bill, and behind on my son Tommie's tuition.

I could imagine what my wife Alice was going to say.

4

"**G**o."

My wife never ceases to amaze me. We've been married for over ten years now, and I would think I know her pretty well. But I don't. Sometimes I think she does it deliberately. 'Cause it seems as if every time I get too complacent, every time I tell myself, "Well, I know how she's gonna react to this one," she throws a curve ball at me.

"What?"

She smiled and shrugged. "Go," she said. "The man's in trouble. He needs your help. You obviously have to go."

I looked at her. "I'm not going to get paid for this."

"I know."

"He offered. I just couldn't take his money."

"Of course."

"I know we're behind on the bills."

She shrugged. "We're always behind on the bills. What's the difference?"

"I guess so," I said.

I was utterly baffled. I was also totally psyched. Alice had foxed me again. What was her game? Was she playing with me? Was she just waiting for me to agree, for me to say, "All right, I have to go," for her to jump up and say, "Oh, no, you're not! You think you're going to Atlantic City by yourself for a vacation, is that what you think? Well, you've got another think coming!" Was that her game? I really didn't know.

I'd told her it was for MacAullif. Alice knew about MacAullif. Not everything, of course. She knew he'd *helped* me in the Darryl Jackson case. She didn't know how deeply he'd involved me in the case, or how close I'd come to getting killed. But she knew MacAullif had befriended me, if you could call it that, and perhaps that's why she thought I owed him the favor.

"I don't know how long I'll be gone," I ventured.

"I know," she said. "But I don't think it will be that long. You're very clever. You'll figure something out."

"Patching up marital disputes is not my forte," I told her.

She smiled. "Well, our marriage is still together. You must be doing something right."

If so, I couldn't figure out what it was. I was really at sea.

"Well," I said. "I guess I'd better start packing."

"I'll help you," she said.

I went in the bedroom and took down a suitcase from the closet shelf. Alice started pulling open drawers and packing underwear, socks and the like.

"Did you tell Richard?" she asked me.

"Not yet."

"Gonna call him?"

I shook my head. "I think I should do it in person. I have to turn in my cases, anyway."

"I see," Alice said. She packed my electric razor. "So you'll just stop in on him on your way."

"Yeah," I said. "But, I could come back."

"Why?"

24

"Well, to see Tommie when he gets home from camp. Say good-bye."

"You can talk to him on the phone," Alice said. "Don't worry about us. We'll be fine."

I was sure they would. However, *I* wasn't doing so well at the moment.

"You're sure you don't mind?" I said.

Alice straightened up, put her hands on her hips, and looked at me as if I were a total idiot.

"It's his *daughter*," she said.

And suddenly I understood. If there's anything Alice is, it's a good mother. And that's what was happening here. That's why she could empathize with MacAullif. MacAullif's *little girl* was in trouble, and something had to be done. Never mind the fact that MacAullif's little girl was a grown woman of twenty-eight, she was still MacAullif's baby, just as Tommie was still Alice's baby, and always would be.

God bless motherhood. I was home free on this one.

Of course, I still had to get around Richard, and that might be a little more difficult.

Richard was a bachelor.

5

"**Y**ou're what?!" Richard screamed in his best you're-ruining-my-life tone of voice. "What did you say?!"

"I'm going to Atlantic City for a few days."

"Today?" Richard cried, his high-pitched voice miraculously managing to rise even higher on the last syllable. "Starting today?"

Richard got up from his desk and began bustling around his office. It was as if someone had just uncapped a bottle marked "Nervous Energy." Richard was a hyperactive little guy who would chew you up and spit you out if you gave him half a chance. Insurance adjusters were generally his meat. But if provoked, he could do a pretty good job on his own investigators.

"You come in here on the spur of the moment, with no notice whatsoever, and tell me you are taking a vacation starting immediately."

"A vacation without pay," I pointed out.

"Without pay? Without pay?" Richard sputtered. "Of course, without pay. You think I want to pay you to go to Atlantic City? Maybe give you a little extra money to gamble? What am I supposed to do while you're gone? You tell me that. Suppose someone breaks his leg in Harlem? What's gonna happen then?"

26

A thought flitted through my mind: suppose a leg breaks in Harlem and there's no investigator there to sign it up—does it make a sound?

I didn't voice the thought. "You have other investigators," I said.

"Yeah, I have other investigators," Richard said. "Part-timers, though. They're never there when you need 'em. Can't count on 'em. You're the only one that I've got I can count on full time."

"If I'm that valuable, maybe I should be making more money," I pointed out.

That almost threw him, but Richard hadn't become a veteran courtroom lawyer without learning how to counter-punch.

"More money? You're making more money right now. That's why I give you cases ahead of the other investigators, because you want to make more money. I do all that for you, and this is the thanks I get."

"It's only for a few days," I said.

"Right," Richard said. "A few days. You can't even tell me how long you're gonna be gone. You want it open-ended. And then I suppose you expect your job will be waiting for you when you get back."

"You have every right to replace me," I said.

That calmed him somewhat. "I have no wish to replace you. You're a perfectly good investigator. I just need you investigating. Not cavorting around Atlantic City somewhere."

"I understand," I said. "I shouldn't be gone long."

Richard got a gleam in his eye. "Wait a minute. Wait a minute. How far is Atlantic City, anyway?"

"I don't know. I've never been there."

"Well, is it in beeper range?"

My heart began to sink.

Richard snatched up the phone and pushed the intercom button. "Hello," he yelped into the phone.

"Yes, of course, it's me, who did you think it was? . . . What's the mileage to Atlantic City? . . . Yes, from here, dammit, where'd you think, from Miami? . . . Well, look it up and call me back." Richard hung up the phone.

"Who was that?" I asked.

Richard shrugged. "Wendy or Cheryl."

I groaned. Wendy and Cheryl were Richard's twin secretaries. I call them twins. I shouldn't. Actually they had only two things in common: their voices and their incompetence. Whichever one of them it had been on the phone, there was no way the mileage she was gonna come up with would be right.

"Well," Richard said. "Perhaps this isn't a total waste. I'm licensed to practice in New Jersey, as you well know. You've signed lots of cases in Jersey. I don't think I've ever had one in Atlantic City, but I'm sure we've had some close to there. So—"

I didn't have to hear what came next. Richard, in his infinite ballsiness, had already decided that since I was gonna be in Atlantic City anyway, I should keep in touch with the office, either by beeper if it was in range, or by calling in periodically if it wasn't, to see if there was any case within the immediate vicinity that I could sign up while I was down there.

By the time Wendy/Cheryl had called back to say that Atlantic City was sixty-nine miles, and therefore within beeper range, which was seventy-five, Richard had his campaign all mapped out. I was his man in Jersey. Johnny on the spot. What a wonderful idea.

It was gonna be one hell of a vacation.

6

I left Richard's office, picked up my car where I'd left it at a meter on Fourteenth Street, went through the Holland Tunnel, and got on the New Jersey Turnpike heading south.

I wasn't setting out absolutely cold. I had hotel reservations. My unexpectedly cooperative wife had called a friend of hers in our building who happened to be a travel agent, and asked her to book me a room. Alice and I had talked it over and figured out that the hotel casinos themselves would be the cheapest place to stay. The theory was that they would charge you next to nothing in order to get you there so they could take your money at their tables. This turned out to be a myth. The casino hotels charged almost twice as much as anyplace else, the theory being let's keep the pikers out and attract the high-rollers who will be the only ones who can afford to stay. The casino hotels were charging a hundred forty to a hundred fifty bucks a night for a single room. Thanks, but no thanks.

The hotel the agent chose for me was the Comfort Inn, at eighty-five a night. It was three miles out of town, and you had to take a courtesy bus in to the casinos. That was fine with me, seeing as how I had a car, and seeing as how the casinos weren't my main concern anyway. Besides, it was in Absecon, which happened to be where MacAullif's daughter lived.

Aside from the hotel reservation, I was going it blind. MacAullif hadn't told me one goddamn useful thing, with the exception of his daughter's address. Even that wasn't gonna help me much, unless I managed to buy a street map somewhere.

All in all, it was a pretty unpromising situation. The best I could figure it was, not having accepted MacAullif's money, after two or three days poking around down there and not having accomplished anything, I could feel justified in reporting back to him what I had managed to learn, and telling him there seemed to be nothing I could do. That, basically, was the height of my expectations. My best-case scenario.

The depth of my expectations, my worst-case scenario, had me running around the outskirts of Atlantic City for three days signing up broken arms and legs for Richard Rosenberg.

However, the odds of that happening were actually poor. See, I have a map of New Jersey—I have to with all the sign-ups I do there. I'd had it right there in my briefcase when Richard had asked me how far it was to Atlantic City, but I hadn't let on. As soon as I got out to my car, however, I whipped the map out and confirmed my suspicions. Sure enough, as I'd thought, there was no way Atlantic City was only sixty-nine miles away. The map didn't list distances from city to city, so there was no way to figure the actual mileage unless I wanted to add up all the five- to ten-mile distances between the little arrows, which I certainly didn't. But it wasn't necessary. Atlantic City was south of Philadelphia. There was no way it was in beeper range.

Which was great. I'd been told to stay on the beeper,

and I'd stay on the beeper, and when I got back and innocently reported that I hadn't been beeped, there'd be nothing Richard could do about it, because it would be Wendy/Cheryl's fault. I'd be the good soldier, just following orders.

I was tooling down the Jersey Pike and gloating over that when my beeper went off. Damn. The best laid plans of mice and men. I checked my watch. It had only been a half hour since I'd left the office. Too soon. There was no way to pretend I was already out of beeper range. I could pretend I'd forgotten to switch it on, but then it would be *my* fault. My best chance was to call in, and hope the beep was just routine and they hadn't discovered the mistake. I cursed Richard, cursed Wendy/Cheryl, shut off the beeper, and pulled into the next Roy Rogers/Bob's Big Boy on the pike.

I called the office, waited for the tone, and punched in my calling card number.

Wendy/Cheryl answered the phone.

"Agent 005."

"Stanley," came the voice of Wendy/Cheryl. "Glad I reached you."

"Oh?" I said, my spirits sinking.

"Yes. I have an assignment for you."

What a relief. Never have I been so happy to get an assignment. I'd knock it off like that, and hustle out of beeper range.

Wendy/Cheryl gave it to me. It wasn't a sign-up. It was a picture assignment. A client had fallen down on the basement steps of a house in Linden, New Jersey, and Richard needed pictures of the broken steps.

I told Wendy/Cheryl I'd take it.

"Fine," she said. "Where are you now?"

"In Elizabeth. Right near there. I'll take care of it."

"Fine. Just be sure you write it down."

31

That was strange. I always write my assignments down. "What do you mean?"

"That you got the assignment in Elizabeth, New Jersey. Richard said to tell you your time and mileage start there. So don't charge him from Manhattan."

I groaned. What a cheap prick. But I wasn't about to argue. I got off the phone fast before anyone thought about the beeper.

I got off the turnpike at the Elizabeth exit and sped down to Linden, which was a whopping four miles on the odometer. It was several more before I found the address, since I didn't have a detailed street map of the area, and there was no answer at the client's phone number Wendy/Cheryl had given me. That wasn't surprising. I figured it was the wrong number anyway.

The address was probably also wrong, but that didn't matter. With the client not answering the phone, there was no way to check it. I'd been assigned it, so it was my job to do it, and if it turned out it wasn't the right address, it wasn't my fault, and I'd get paid for it anyway.

But the main thing was getting it done so I'd be off the hook and could head south. I asked directions four times, and half an hour later found myself cruising down the street where the client, one Raymon Ortega, presumably was injured.

One of the things about Richard's clients is, a lot of 'em don't have any money, and the neighborhoods they live in leave a lot to be desired. This neighborhood was no exception. The houses were in remarkably poor repair, and the one I wanted was the worst of the lot. It was a two-story frame house that had presumably once been white with green trim. The most recent coat of paint was at least twenty years old, and had not worn well. The shutters, those that remained, dangled, sometimes by a single screw. Most of the panes of glass in the curtainless windows were broken. And the front door looked suspiciously as if it would fall off the hinges the moment I knocked on it.

It didn't, however. In fact it was quite solid. It was also locked. And no matter how loud I pounded, no one came to open it.

I know a TV detective can open a door with a hat pin. I can't. The only way I know to deal with a locked door is to stand in front of it and look stupid.

I stood in front of the door looking stupid and pondering my next move. I've had situations like this before in the course of my job, so I know how to deal with them. And the way you deal with them is, if there's any way possible, you do the assignment. You do it because (1) you won't get paid for it until it's done, and (2) you don't want to come back.

So I circled the house, looking for a way in. A cellar door, one of those connected to the house at a forty-five degree angle, looked promising, but proved to be locked. However, I found I was able to walk up it and reach the window in the wall above. Since a pane of glass was missing, it was a simple matter to reach in, unlock and raise the window. I did so, climbed up and dropped through.

I found myself in a kitchen that bore no signs of human occupancy. There was dirt, filth and rotten garbage everywhere. I'd have been willing to bet no one had lived here for years. But that wasn't my fault. I didn't know when the accident had happened. As far as I knew, this was the house and I was gonna take the damn pictures.

I went to what I presumed was the door to the cellar. It was. I tried the light switch just inside the door. As expected, nothing happened. And it was pitch dark in the basement. That made no difference in terms of the pictures—with the flash my Cannon

Snappy 50 can shoot in the dark—but it made a difference to me. After all, as far as I knew, one person had already broken a leg on these stairs.

I went down the stairs very cautiously. There was a handrail, but I couldn't really see it, and I couldn't count on it not to give out on me halfway down.

I reached the bottom. I heaved a sigh of relief and grabbed my camera, which was hanging under my coat by a strap over my shoulder and around my neck. I snapped on the flash, took two steps back to get the right angle. And took a shot of the stairs.

He was standing in the shadows by the stair well. The flash lit him up in bold relief, made him look larger than life and scary as hell.

He would have looked scary anyway. He had bushy black hair, a bristling black beard and wild, glowing eyes. I know part of it was the flash, but I swear his eyes would have glowed on their own. He was dressed in what could best be described as rags. They weren't, they were clothes, but they were so covered with dirt and grease that it was impossible, for instance, to say if the shirt was solid or plaid. The face was also covered with dirt and grease. As were the hands.

It was the hands that caught my attention. To be more precise, it was the right hand.

That was the one holding the knife.

"What the fuck you want?" he growled.

What I wanted was to get out of there alive. I didn't express the thought, however. Instead I tried to keep from peeing in my pants and tried to think of what to say.

You see, there was nothing I could *do*. As I said, I don't carry a gun or any other means of protection. The only thing I have going for me in an emergency is my quick wit.

Which seemed to have deserted me. My mind was

racing. I tried to see the situation from his point of view. I was wearing a suit and tie—I always do when I'm on the job—so there were only two things the guy could think: I was either a cop or a damn fool.

I was so scared I couldn't think of a thing to say. Which is why I resorted to the truth.

"You own this building?" I blurted.

He gawked at me. "Fuck no."

"Then you got nothing to worry about," I said. "I'm a private detective, and I'm employed to take pictures of these stairs so some guy named Raymon Ortega can sue the owner and make a shitload of money."

The minute I said the word "money" I made a face like a golfer who'd just topped a drive. What a stupid thought to put in his head. *Money*. The guy's eyes gleamed even more when I said it. And now his lips parted in a hideous grin, revealing gleaming, pearly white teeth.

And then he started for me.

For a second I thought I was going to faint.

And then he was on me, reaching out and grabbing, and—

He pumped my hand up and down, grinning like a zany, as if his face was going to crack. "Me! Me!" he said, nodding and grinning. "You work for me! Me! Raymon Ortega!"

I couldn't believe it. Wendy/Cheryl had gotten one right.

7

I got beeped again before I even got back on the Jersey Turnpike. I called in and Wendy/Cheryl gave me a picture assignment to shoot a broken sidewalk in Rahway. I shot it, got beeped again, and was directed to shoot a defective swing in a public playground in Perth Amboy.

By now even a dunce like me had figured out what was going on. Richard, pissed off at the thought of my leaving him in the lurch, had sent the paralegals to the files to pull out every old pending photo assignment they could find in New Jersey. I didn't care, just as long as it kept them all too busy to think about the beeper range.

I shot the defective swing (which had long since been fixed, but that wasn't my problem), got on the Garden State Parkway, and drove like the wind out of beeper range.

Atlantic City is about one hundred twenty miles from New York, if you're keeping count. I was, and I loved it. Seventy-five miles is just the maximum limit they guarantee the beeper will work. It'll go further than that. But over a hundred, no way.

I got off the Garden State Parkway at Exit 40, and

cruised down 30 East with the blessed sound of silence in my ears.

My hotel was on Route 30, just a few miles down the road in Absecon, right where the travel agent had said it would be. It was 5:30 when I checked in. Richard's office was still open—Wendy and Cheryl stay on the phones until six—but they weren't beeping me. What a surprise.

I registered at the desk, lugged my suitcase up to the room. I went back downstairs and asked the girl at the desk if she knew where Traymore Avenue was. She certainly did. It turned out it was just about a mile from the hotel, back up 30 the way I'd come and turn right at the MacDonald's. I didn't even have to buy a map.

I went out, hopped in my car and drove over there. The address turned out to be your basic two-story middle-income house and yard on a pleasant tree-lined street of similar structures. The double-door of the two-car garage was closed, so presumably both vehicles were in, although I couldn't tell. It wasn't dark enough yet for lights to be on, so I couldn't really see anything through the windows, though, to be perfectly honest, I didn't really want to. I figured there was nothing to do tonight, anyway. All I wanted to do was verify the address and familiarize myself with the house. I figured to start in the morning.

The question nagging at me, of course, was: start what? I figured the question would keep for the morning, however.

Meanwhile, hey! Here I was in Atlantic City. I'd never been in Atlantic City. But I'd certainly heard enough about it, what with New Yorkers always talking about it, and what with all those ads on TV. And I figured, hey, if Harold was mixed up in something shady, what would be more logical than that it would have to do with gambling?

I thought about that some, and then I went out and had some dinner, and then I thought about it some more, and the long and the short of it was before too long I talked myself into the notion that it would be a pretty good idea for me to familiarize myself with the local casinos.

With this virtuous idea in mind, I bought a street map for a buck fifty from a vending machine in the hotel lobby, and headed out for playland.

It turned out the street map was entirely unnecessary. When I got back out to the back parking lot, I could see them there, lit up against the sky across the bay. Tall buildings with neon lights on top. Could this be it? Could this be the city of gold?

I got in my car and headed out. Screw the map. It looked like 30 East would get me there, so that's what I took. Immediately I was assaulted by signs. "BEST NAME IN GAMING FOR FIFTY YEARS.—HARRAH'S." "HOLLYWOOD EXHIBIT—FREE ADMISSION—SANDS." "MEET BUCK BUSTER—THE DOLLAR SLOTBUSTER'S BEST FRIEND.—CAESAR'S." And the buildings were getting closer and closer across the bay. "BEST NAME IN SLOTS—BALLY'S." "120,000 IN JACKPOTS PAID HOURLY—RESORTS."

I followed the flow of traffic, and before I knew it I was driving down Atlantic Avenue, and all the casino hotels were coming up on my left. Signs were now proclaiming free parking in this city of gold. I succumbed to the lure, hung a left, and soon found myself in the parking lot of Bally's Park Place Hotel and Casino. The attendant took my car key, gave me a ticket and told me to have it validated by the cashier so as I wouldn't have to pay him for the parking. I thought that was right nice of him.

I came out of the parking lot, wondering which way to go. Silly me. Follow the people, follow the signs. I did, went in a door, down a hall, turned left and suddenly there it was. I was looking at it.

I was astounded. I had expected a room. It was the size of a football stadium. A vast sea of gambling machines stretched out in front of me. Slot machines. One-armed bandits. And every single one of them seemed to be taken. Mostly by women. And mostly old.

I wandered through the sea. In the center of the room I found the traditional gambling games. Blackjack, roulette, and craps. About half of the tables were filled. I figured that was because it was midweek. Weekends they'd probably be solid.

I watched for a while. It was kind of interesting. At the crap table everyone was animated. The guys around the table were all talking to each other and shoving out bets. And the guy with the dice was talking to 'em as if he thought that would help. Or perhaps he'd seen a movie somewhere where crap shooters talked to dice. At any rate, he was doing it.

Blackjack tables were different. I watched one where no one said a word. They just pointed. They pushed out their bets. The dealer would silently shove the cards out of the shoe, then look at the players in turn. If they wanted a hit, they'd point to their cards. If they didn't, they'd wave their hand palm down over them. The dealer'd then face his hole card, deal himself cards if required, then silently pay out or collect all the bets.

The activity at the roulette wheels lay somewhere between these extremes. Players would talk, of course, as they couldn't reach the whole betting board, and had to tell the croupier on what numbers to slide their chips. But it was much more refined, genteel, low key.

Even big wins were accepted with smug smiles rather than whoops of joy. Losses caused merely a raised eyebrow and shake of the head.

I felt like participating. I mean, if you come to Atlantic City, you should gamble a little. I also knew I'd lose my shirt. I've never played craps in my life. The only blackjack I'd ever played was for fun with friends at college, and I'd always lost.

I'd played roulette once. That was the only time in my life I'd ever been in a casino. That was an illegal casino, though. This was my first time in a legal one. In the illegal casino I'd lost fifty dollars. That time, of course, the wheel had probably been rigged. I figured the wheels in here probably weren't. I also figured it probably wouldn't make any difference. The odds are for the house, so eventually you're going to lose, one way or another.

The other thing was, all the tables, blackjack, craps and roulette, had a five dollar minimum bet. On my travel budget, that was just too steep. There was no way I was parting with that kind of money.

I wanted to do something, though, so I bought a roll of quarters and started playing the slots. It wasn't that easy to do. The old ladies had 'em pretty well locked up. Oh, to be fair, there were some young ladies and some men, too, both old and young. But they were the exception. But the older ladies, middle-aged and up, were the rule.

About four aisles down I spotted a free machine about halfway down the row. I slid in next to it.

The woman at the machine next to me, who had just pulled the lever and set her wheels spinning, turned on me savagely.

"That's mine!" she snarled.

I looked down and saw that the payoff slot was full of quarters. The woman grabbed a handful out of the slot, fed five of them into the machine, pulled the lever and, without waiting to see the result, hopped back to the other machine, repeating the process.

I was amazed. The woman was compulsively, methodically and without a scrap of enjoyment, playing both machines.

As I continued my tour of the floor I discovered that this was by no means rare. Many women were playing two machines. Some were playing three.

I found what appeared to be an unoccupied machine. I stalked it carefully. Determined it to be unmarked by any tigress's scent. I shoved quarters into it with minimal expectations and minimal results. It was fun watching the wheels revolve, but that was about it. Occasionally I hit a small payoff, ten quarters, twenty quarters max.

I put my quarters into one of the plastic cups that were stacked next to each machine for that very purpose, and wandered around the floor, stopping now and then to play what looked like an interesting machine.

Eventually, having fed all my quarters into one machine or another, I reached the back of the room. The sign over the door said, "Exit to Boardwalk." That looked good to me. I went through the doors and out.

I strolled down the Boardwalk. I liked it. For one thing, it was made of boards. I know that seems logical, but it didn't necessarily have to be. The fact that it was was nice.

To my left was the beach and the ocean. To my right were the ice cream parlors and souvenir shops and penny arcades. And casino hotels.

I went past Caesar's Palace. I'd heard of Caesar's Palace, so I went in to check it out. Very much like Bally's. Huge room, lots of machines, lots of old women.

I bought some quarters, strolled around the casino floor, played some slots, checked out the layout.

I went back outside and walked down the Boardwalk. I stopped in at all the casino hotels. I didn't gamble though, didn't let myself get sucked in. Just checked out the layouts and piddled around with the slots.

The last hotel on the strip was the Golden Nugget. I thought of the TV ads as I walked in. I didn't see Frank Sinatra, though. I didn't see Kenny Rogers or Dolly Parton, either. I didn't even see Steve.

I left the Golden Nugget and strolled back down the Boardwalk to Bally's. It was a long walk, but pleasant. I passed it up and continued on to the casinos on the other side. I did them, then strolled back.

In Bally's I had one of the cashiers validate my parking ticket. She seemed happy to do it.

I went back to the parking lot and got my car. They gave it to me free. God bless gambling.

I pulled out, stopped and checked my map. I discovered there were two casinos I'd missed. Harrah's and Trump Castle. That's because those two weren't on the Boardwalk with the others, but were a little further north around the tip of the bay. Seeing as how I had no idea where Harold might like to hang out, I decided to check 'em out too.

I followed the signs to Trump Castle. There was a free parking garage. I spiraled around and around up to the third level and found a space. "Free Parking, No Validation Necessary," the sign said. I liked that.

Trump Castle advertises too, and I wondered if I would feel like the king of the castle.

I took the elevator down from the parking garage and the elevator up to the main floor and walked into the casino. It seemed to be much the same layout.

I bought some quarters, checked out the layout, and piddled around with the slots.

I'd just fed my last quarter into my last machine when it suddenly hit me. *I'd bought eight rolls of quarters! That's eighty bucks!* I couldn't believe it. There I was, so afraid I'd lose fifty bucks at roulette, and I'd just pissed away eighty at the slots!

I stood there, in the center of Trump Castle Hotel and Casino, as waves of nausea engulfed me. Believe it or not, I didn't feel like the king of the castle.

I felt like a fucking asshole.

I got into my car and drove straight back to my hotel before I got into any more trouble. To be honest, I didn't feel truly safe until I got back into my room.

The light on my telephone was on, indicating there was a message at the desk. Shit. I realized, in all my excitement or lack of it, I'd forgotten to call Alice. And it was too late to call her now. I called the front desk to pick up the message.

It wasn't from Alice. It was the final kick in the teeth, and somehow a fitting end to that draggy day.

The message was to call Rosenberg & Stone the next morning at nine o'clock sharp.

8

I got up early the next morning, drove out to Traymore Avenue and staked out the house. I felt like a damn fool. For me this was nothing new. Feeling like a damn fool, I mean. Staking out houses was a little out of my line. But I was doing it for MacAullif, and I knew it was important to him, so, stupid as I thought it was, I tried to make a good job of it.

Green as I am at this game, I did know one thing. When you're following someone, you can't sit right outside their front door. The object is not to be seen.

Across the street, two houses down, I found the perfect spot. A big oak tree by the side of a driveway overhung the road. Pulling in under the overhanging branches, I could be protected both from the sun and from a casual glance from across the street.

I pulled into the spot to test the theory. It looked good to me. The car was facing away from the house, so I wouldn't be sitting there staring at it. But by angling the rear-view mirror slightly, I could frame the front door of the house and be able to see who went in and out without having to look around. Moreover, the car was now pointing back towards town, in the direction in which I assumed Harold would be going. It was perfect.

I checked my watch. Seven o'clock. I figured there wouldn't be any activity before eight A.M. at the earliest, but I'd wanted to make sure. I sat in the car, sipping coffee and trying to convince myself that I was a TV detective on an important stakeout. It didn't work. The thing is, on TV you never see a detective sit in a car for hours. After all, they only got an hour to solve the whole case. At worst, you get a time-dissolve, and then the quarry emerges from the house.

In real life it doesn't work that way. I sat there sipping coffee and looking in the rear-view mirror, and by eight o'clock I was bored silly, I had a stiff neck, and I had to take a terrific piss.

The front door opened at 8:05. I was all tensed up and ready to go, but it wasn't Harold. It was Barbara and the kid.

MacAullif had given me a snapshot of Barbara and Harold, which would have been helpful in case I'd happened to confuse them with some *other* young couple with a seven-year-old kid who happened to live at the same address, which gives you some idea of MacAullif's estimation of my detective skills.

I must say the picture didn't do her justice. Barbara MacAullif Dunleavy was a knockout. Short brown hair, round pink cheeks, soft eyes, and a figure that wouldn't quit, as a tough detective would say. And all of that through the rear-view mirror. I would have loved to have turned around and taken a better look, but my prudence and/or cowardice forbade it.

The kid was cute too, by the way, but then, all seven-year-old kids are. The mom was something else. Jesus Christ, I thought, so this is MacAullif's daughter. Who would have thought it?

Barbara went to the garage and swung up the huge double door. Inside were a Chevy station wagon and a Mercedes convertible. I knew Barbara and the kid were going to get into the wagon. They did. I cursed Harold Dunleavy for a sexist pig. Barbara would have looked great in the convertible.

The station wagon pulled out of the driveway, hung a left, passed me and drove on down the street.

O.K., ace detective, put that down in your notebook: "8:05—mother drives kid to school."

I sat there, feeling stupider by the minute. It didn't help, having to take that piss.

At 8:25 the front door opened and a man came out. About thirty, 5'10", one hundred sixty pounds, dark hair, blue eyes. I checked the photograph. Son of a bitch. It was him. Harold Dunleavy. The perpetrator himself. I'd done it. I'd identified him.

Harold Dunleavy got in his car, pulled out of the driveway, turned left, drove past me, and headed back toward town. I gave him a head start, then pulled out and tagged along.

There's a trick to following someone in a car. Unfortunately, I don't know it. However, in this instance, there was a saving grace. A stockbroker living in the suburbs with his wife and kid doesn't expect to be tailed on his way to work.

Harold drove into downtown Atlantic City, drove down Atlantic Avenue and pulled into a parking lot. I was lucky to find a meter. The meter said no parking between eight and nine A.M. It was only 8:45, but I figured I couldn't be fussy. I also figured if I got a ticket it would serve me right.

Harold came out of the parking lot, crossed the street and went into an office building.

I whipped out my pocket notebook and checked. Sure enough, that was the address MacAullif had given me for Harold's firm.

I didn't follow Harold into the building. I didn't want him to see me, and there would have been no point. I just stood on the sidewalk, cursing Harold, cursing MacAullif and cursing myself.

I stomped off to a diner down the street, went in the men's room, took the piss of my life and stomped back out again, without even feeling guilty that I hadn't ordered anything.

There was a pay phone on the corner across from the office building. I went to it and called Rosenberg & Stone.

Wendy/Cheryl answered the phone. "Good morning, Stanley, right on time," she said.

"I believe in punctuality," I told her.

"You went out of beeper range," she said accusingly, as if that were my fault. "Richard was furious. We had to stay late last night and call every hotel in town."

"I'm glad you found me," I lied.

"Yes, but it's a real nuisance, having you out of beeper range. Richard wants you to call in four times a day, at nine, twelve, three and five."

"I'll set my watch."

"What?"

"No problem. You got anything for me?"

She did. Two more photo assignments, vaguely in the area, confirming my suspicion that Richard was paying me back by loading me up with the shit. I didn't care. Having figured out what was going on, I knew there was nothing urgent about the photo assignments, so it didn't matter when I did 'em. I figured I'd knock off as many as I could on my way back. I certainly couldn't do 'em now. Not while I was on this terribly important assignment.

I got off the phone with Wendy/Cheryl and called Alice. Predictably, she was pissed I hadn't called her the night before, but delighted to discover I wasn't dead.

I told her about my adventures in the casinos. She voiced the opinion that I was an ignoramus. I had to concur. I promised her I would lay off gambling and concentrate on the very important MacAullif's daughter case. I also told her I was defraying my expenses by knocking off photo assignments for Richard. That mollified her somewhat. I was glad. It sure as hell didn't mollify me.

I got off the phone and went back to take up my vigil. Nothing much seemed to be happening. The front of Harold's office building looked pretty much the same as it had when he'd gone in.

For lack of anything better to do I checked my car. I hadn't gotten a ticket, but the parking meter was beginning to look hungry.

I checked it out, something I hadn't bothered to do when I'd been keeping Harold in sight.

It was an hour meter. It said: "1 dime = 30 minutes." Underneath it said: "For your convenience: 1 quarter = 1 hour."

I blinked. I looked again. Yes, I'd read it right. Only in Atlantic City, where all machines are *designed* to rip people off, could you consider it convenient to be ripped off for a nickel.

I fished in my pocket. All I had was quarters. I didn't have any dimes.

I was pissed off at the parking meter, and I didn't want to give in.

There was a newsstand across the street. I figured I could run in there, give 'em two quarters and ask for five dimes. But I figured if I did, Harold would probably come out and I'd miss him. Besides, the guy probably wouldn't give 'em to me unless I bought something. I'd have to buy a candy bar to get change. I didn't want a candy bar.

Shit.

I put a quarter in the meter. I felt like an asshole.

Three quarters later Harold emerged from the building with another young man, similarly dressed in suit and tie.

I followed them two blocks down Atlantic Avenue, where they went into a restaurant. Gee, I thought. I think I can figure this one out.

Forty-five minutes later they emerged, walked back to Harold's office building and went in. I was glad. It was just time for me to shove another quarter in the meter.

It was about 2:30 and I was really getting fed up when Harold came out of the building again. This time he was alone. He set off down Atlantic Avenue.

I still had a good half hour on the meter, but I didn't know how long this was going to take, so I shoved another quarter in just to be sure, and set off after him.

Harold walked about a half dozen blocks and then turned onto Tennessee Avenue, heading south. My pulse quickened. Great. He was heading for the Boardwalk and the casinos.

Two doors down the street, however, he went into an office building. I couldn't go into the lobby with him, of course, so I watched from across the street until he got into the elevator. As soon as the elevator doors closed, I raced across the street and into the lobby.

I watched the elevator indicator to see which floor he got off. Unfortunately, that turned out to be another one of those things that works great in the movies but sucks in real life. There'd been people in the elevator with him, and the elevator stopped on four of the five floors.

I checked the call board in the lobby. The tenants in

the building were largely lawyers, real estate brokers and, yes, stockbrokers.

I waited outside the building for forty-five minutes. Toward the end I started getting antsy, wondering if I was going to get a parking ticket on top of everything else. Then Harold came out again. He walked right back to Atlantic Avenue, back to his building and in.

I fed another quarter into the parking meter.

I considered strangling MacAullif.

Five o'clock, Harold emerged from the building, went to the parking lot and got his car. I wondered who'd paid more for his parking, Harold with his lot or me with my quarters.

I followed Harold up Route 30 back to Absecon and home.

The double doors to the garage were open and the station wagon was already inside. Harold pulled in beside it, got out of the car, pulled the double doors down, and locked the garage.

I figured Harold was through for the night.

I figured I was too. Jesus Christ.

I went back to the hotel and called MacAullif. He didn't seem a bit disappointed with my report.

"Ninety percent of surveillance is waiting," MacAullif said. "We do it all the time. Just stick with it. You're doing fine."

I hung up the phone and called Rosenberg & Stone for the fourth time that day. They seemed to have run out of moldy photo assignments. I assured Wendy/ Cheryl I was on the job, promised to call first thing in the morning and hung up.

I called Alice. I got to talk to Tommie about camp. Swimming had been great, but they hadn't played baseball.

Alice got back on the phone. I told her what I'd

accomplished. As usual, she was sympathetic and supportive.

"So, what are you doing tonight?" she asked.

I hadn't even thought of it. I told her so.

"I hope you're not going to gamble," she said.

I told her I thought I'd had my fill.

I hung up the phone and lay down on the bed, exhausted. Jesus, what a day of doing nothing. All right, what the hell *am* I gonna do tonight? I mean, here I am, footloose and fancy free in Atlantic City, with the evening stretched out before me. Aside from gambling, what sort of pleasures could a gentleman seek?

The thing is, I'm not the type of guy to cheat on my wife. Now please don't take that to be any chest-thumping declaration of overwhelming virtue on my part. True, I'm a happily married man and I love my wife and kid and all that, but that's not the only reason. The fact is, I am scared to death of women. They are an inscrutable species. I don't understand them. In my opinion, any guy who claims he understands women is either a fool or a liar. Oh, sure, some guy may be considered a great ass-man and do *well* with women, but understand them—I don't think so. Women are incredible creatures. They have an almost magical quality. I don't know what it is—if I did, it wouldn't be magical—but they have it. And they all have it, from my wife right on down to the gum-chewing ticket seller in the movie theater.

So chasing after women isn't quite my style. Oh, that's not to say I haven't thought about it. Like Jimmy Carter, I have lusted in my heart many times. I have my fantasies. One of them has always been becoming so successful a writer that starlets and groupies and what-have-you were constantly throwing themselves at my feet. This is a very pleasant fantasy. My wife and kid don't enter into it, incidently. In the fantasy, they just conveniently aren't there. That's the nice thing about a fantasy. Reality doesn't have to intrude.

That particular fantasy sustained me for many years. Then along came AIDS.

I must say, I resent AIDS. I realize that's an incredibly boorish and insensitive statement, sort of on a par with saying, "Lepers make me nervous." But it happens to be the truth. I resent AIDS. I mean, here's a reality so harsh, so cruel, so brutal and so graphic that it *does* intrude on the fantasy. And that's the unkindest cut of all.

I remember back in the days when sex was young and innocent. It used to be, if you had sex, you might get the clap, in which case you'd get a shot and have to take it easy for a week. Then it got a little worse: if you had sex, you might get herpes—you couldn't get rid of it, but it wasn't that bad: a lot of people had it, and you could all kind of itch together.

Now, you have sex and you die.

AIDS has gotten so frightening they're even advertising condoms on TV. To me, this is mindboggling. When I was a kid, you couldn't even *find* a condom. Druggists kept them hidden under the counter. If you wanted one, you had to ask for it. For a pimply-faced kid, that took a lot of guts. And you'll recall, I was never long on guts.

They didn't call them condoms then, either. We kids called 'em rubbers, of course, but that was slang. The proper names were contraceptives (for prevention of pregnancy), or prophylactics (for prevention of disease). A contraceptive or prophylactic or rubber was like a thin, transparent balloon. One looked at it and thought, "Jesus Christ, this is the only thing standing between me knocking up some girl, dropping out of school and fucking up my entire life?" And then one usually wound up filling the damn thing up with water and dropping it out the window on a passing classmate, which, while not quite as much fun as having sex, was infinitely safer.

But that was contraceptives and prophylactics. Today we have condoms, which I hope would be tougher, seeing as how they have a more important job to do, keeping you from getting dead. They seem tougher, somehow. Even the name sounds tougher. CON-DOM. It sounds like a steel-belted radial. It inspires confidence. CON-DOM.

I can recall back in my youth, on one of those few occasions when I did actually wind up having sex, I used *two* contraceptives, just to be sure. I'm sure I only would have needed one condom.

At any rate, I wasn't going to be chasing any women in Atlantic City. Because, when the cowards line up to be counted, they can count me in. And I'll tell you something. In this new AIDS society we live in, they can talk about safe sex all they like. But I am such a big coward that, as far as I'm concerned, in my opinion, the only truly safe sex is masturbation.

With a condom.

I went to the movies.

9

Next morning, bright and early, feeling like a complete asshole, I drove out to take up my vigil in front of the Dunleavy house.

I cruised by the house slowly at ten of eight. The garage doors were closed, both cars presumably still inside.

I drove on by to take up my position under the oak tree. Only I couldn't do it. There was a car parked right in the spot. Great, I thought. What else can go wrong?

I drove on by, hung a right, drove around the block, and came up on the house again. This time, instead of driving past it, I stopped a few houses down the other way. It wasn't nearly as good a position. In the first place, there was no overhanging tree to shield me. In the second place, I had to look straight out the window to see the house, instead of being able to glance into the rear-view mirror. But beggars can't be choosers. Besides, by now I figured I had the routine down fairly well.

Sure enough, 8:05, Barbara and the kid came out, opened the garage doors, got in the station wagon and pulled out.

Hot stuff. Log it in the notebook.

I watched the station wagon drive off. As it went by, the car that had been parked under the oak tree in my spot pulled out and drove off too.

Coincidence?

Maybe.

Maybe not.

Well, fuck Harold, I thought. Odds were he was just going to work anyway.

I pulled out and tagged along.

It took less than half a mile to confirm my suspicions. During that stretch the station wagon made five or six turns. The car that had been parked in my spot made them too. So did I, for that matter.

We made quite a procession. It seemed like overkill, somehow, the three of us, all driving one kid to school.

The car I was following was a nondescript, beat-up Chevy of a bluish color, not too old, not too new, just the sort of thing a real detective would drive. I couldn't see the guy driving it very well, just the back of his head, which was enough to tell me he had dark hair and was bald on top. I hoped to hell he wouldn't spot me. I realized there was no reason that he should. After all, he was concentrating on following the girl. He had no reason to suspect *he* was wearing a tail.

The station wagon pulled up in front of an elementary school, and the kid got out and went in. The station wagon drove off. The driver of the Chevy and I, who had been discreetly parked half a block and a block, respectively, down the road, pulled out and gave chase.

The station wagon went through a series of turns, and I realized we were headed back the way we'd come. Sure enough, ten minutes later we wound up back at the house.

Barbara pulled back into the garage. Harold's car

was already gone. I figured he'd gone to work. At least, I certainly hoped he had.

The Chevy went on by and took up its station under the oak tree again. I stopped toward the other end of the block, as before.

Barbara got out of the car and went into the house.

We sat there for two hours.

Nothing happened. Absolutely nothing. I felt like going down to the Chevy and asking the guy, "Would you like to play some gin rummy while we wait?" I rejected the notion.

I had just realized I had forgotten to call Rosenberg & Stone this morning and was now in deep shit, when a truck came down the street and stopped in front of the Dunleavy house. The letters on the door said, "JOHNSON'S TREE SURGEONS." I thought it would be neat if it turned out the oak tree my buddy in the Chevy had aced me out of had Dutch elm disease, and the guy in the truck pruned it all away.

It didn't happen. The guy got out of the truck. He was a young guy, early twenties, with blond, curly hair, wearing a white t-shirt and blue jeans. He looked tanned and healthy. He went up to the front door of the Dunleavy house and rang the bell. The door opened, and he went in.

My friend in the Chevy got out of his car. He looked around him, somewhat furtively, I thought. He couldn't see me, scrunched down in the front seat of my car. But I could see him. He had a thin face, with a thin, hawk nose, and somewhat protruding lips. He reminded me of a weasel.

When he was certain no one was watching him, he crossed the street. Then he began strolling casually toward the Dunleavy house. Before he got there, he took a look all around him, then ducked around the side of the house to the back.

I got out of my car and crossed the street. I walked quickly down to the Dunleavy house. As I walked by the far corner, I glanced in the direction my buddy had gone. There was no sign of him. He had disappeared around back.

I didn't want the guy to see me, but I sure as hell wanted to know what he was trying to do. I figured the backyards of the houses must all connect, so I walked past the next house and then detoured into its backyard.

There were fences, as I'd figured, but you could see over 'em and through 'em. Two fences away, there was my buddy the Weasel, standing on his tiptoes and peering into a back window of the Dunleavy house.

I stood there and watched. I hoped nobody would come out the back door of the house and yell at me. Fortunately, nobody did. I wouldn't have minded if someone had come out the back door and yelled at the Weasel. In fact, it might have been even kind of fun. But nobody did that, either.

After a while, something must have happened. I could tell, 'cause the Weasel started getting excited. He stopped looking in the window and started looking all around him. He spotted an apple box under the back porch. He pulled it out, dragged it over to the window. He stood up on it. I saw him take something out of his jacket pocket. He held it up to his eye, which was now level with the window.

Now I've had bum hunches before, and my luck as a gambler hadn't been too good this trip, but I'd have been willing to bet you a nickel he was taking pictures.

After a while, the Weasel stuck the presumed camera back in his jacket, hopped down from the box, stashed the box back under the porch, and scuttled out from behind the house.

I crept along the side of my house to the front. Just

as I got there, the Weasel came darting across the street to his car. He hopped in and pulled out.

I had to run to my car, too. The Weasel was going at a good clip, and I didn't want to let him get away.

The Weasel got onto 30 East, heading for downtown Atlantic City. He drove to Atlantic Avenue, pulled into a meter, and got out. I pulled up next to a fire plug half a block away and watched. Either there was time on the meter, or the Weasel was willing to take a chance, 'cause he didn't put any money in it. He got out of the car carrying what looked to me like a camera bag, and went into a Photomat.

Thinking about the meter started associations in my mind, made me realize I was only a few blocks away from Harold's office. I wondered if he was in it.

The Weasel came back out of the Photomat, got in his car and pulled out. I pulled out and tagged along behind.

In midtown stop-and-go traffic there was nothing suspicious about my being right behind him, so I was able to pull up close and get his license number. I wrote it down.

The Weasel kept on going out Atlantic Avenue. I had no idea where he was going, and I didn't really care, unless it was back to the Dunleavy house. The direction he was going said he wasn't. Every block seemed to confirm the opinion. I followed him until Atlantic Avenue turned into Ventnor, followed him another twenty blocks, and let it go at that.

I turned around and drove back to Absecon, to the Dunleavy house. The tree surgeon's truck was gone. The station wagon was still there.

I had a notion to go up and ring the front doorbell. "Excuse me, miss, I'm taking a survey, and—" I quickly put it out of my mind. MacAullif didn't want that, and I didn't want that. The low profile, the man on the periphery, that's me.

I turned around, drove back to Atlantic City, and took up my station in front of Harold's office.

I called Rosenberg & Stone. Wendy/Cheryl was hopping mad. She bawled me out for a couple of minutes, then put me on hold. A minute later, Richard Rosenberg's voice exploded in my ear.

"What the hell do you think you're doing?" he screamed. "I tell you to call in, I *want* you to call in! You don't do it, you're losing me business, you're costing me money, you're a drain on the firm—"

He went on in that vein for some time, then gave me back to Wendy/Cheryl to get my assignments.

There were none. My not calling in had had no effect on anything. It was just the principle of the thing.

I hung up and called MacAullif.

"Anything stirring?" he asked.

"Maybe a little. I want you to trace a license plate number for me."

"You got something?"

"Yeah, but it's not what you want."

"What?"

"It appears I'm not the only game in town."

"What the hell is that supposed to mean?"

"I think there's another detective on the case."

"What!?"

"I think there's—"

"I heard you, I heard you. What the hell are you talking about?"

"I spotted another tail."

"You're kidding! On Harold?"

"No. On your daughter."

"What the hell!"

"I don't make the news, I just report it. The best I can determine, there is a private detective following your daughter. He tailed her this morning when she took the kid to school. He kept her under surveillance until she went home. At present he seems to have quit."

I couldn't tell MacAullif about the pictures and the tree surgeon. I didn't have the heart. I know he's a cop and all that, but he's also a father, and I figured there's some things a father just doesn't want to hear.

"So what's the idea?" said MacAullif.

"I don't know. I'm just reporting the facts. The thing is, I figure the guy must be a private dick, and I'd like to confirm it and tag who he is. So can you trace the license number?"

"It's a Jersey plate?"

"Yeah."

"That makes it harder."

"Sure, but you got connections. I'm sure you can do it. Just pull a few strings. It's your daughter, for Christ's sake."

"I know, I know," MacAullif said. "Yeah, I can do it. It's just I don't want anyone knowing about it."

"O.K., get on it," I said. "I'll call you back in half an hour."

"I don't know if I can do it that fast."

"Give it a try."

MacAullif gave it a good one. When I called back a half an hour later he had the information. The car was registered to a Joseph T. Steerwell. MacAullif gave me the guy's address, and it was the direction I'd seen him driving off in. He also gave me his phone number, height, weight, birth date—the whole shmear. The description fit close enough. It was the Weasel all right.

And he was a licensed private detective.

10

I must admit (and often do) that as a private detective I leave a lot to be desired. I am not the swiftest thing in the world. In fact, I am often pretty slow on the uptake, and I have a problem sometimes putting two and two together and making four. So I must confess, it was not until after I got off the phone with MacAullif that I got an idea any other detective would have had years ago.

The address MacAullif had given me for the Weasel would be his home address.

Not the address of his office.

I walked over to Tennessee Avenue and went to the building where I'd trailed Harold the day before. I went inside and looked at the call board. Sure enough, there on the fourth floor, hidden in among all the lawyers and stockbrokers and real estate agents, was the Minton Detective Agency.

I got in the elevator and went up to the fourth floor. I walked down the hall and found 421. It looked like a detective agency. It had a frosted glass door like the ones you see in the movies. My office in Manhattan has a door of solid wood. I always think of it as one of my failings.

I pushed the door open and walked in. I found

myself in a small reception area with doors leading off from it. A matronly secretary was sitting at a desk typing something. She continued typing without looking up. I figured she was just trying to get to the end of the line. I waited.

I waited long enough for her to have gotten to the end of several lines. When she started in on a new paragraph, I said, "Excuse me."

She murmured, "Ah, shit!" grabbed an eraser, and glared at me. "Yes," she hissed.

I gave her my best smile. "Joe Steerwell?"

"Out for the day," she snapped, and immediately turned to attack the page in the typewriter.

I went out the door, wondering if the secretary could be considered an improvement over Wendy and Cheryl or just a change. I decided I would have to observe her for accuracy before I could make a proper judgment.

I also went out with my obvious theory having been tested and having proven true.

Harold Dunleavy had hired the Weasel to spy on his wife.

I went back to my post outside Harold's office and called MacAullif.

He was surprised to hear from me again so soon.

"Hey, I'm interested and all that," he said, "but I happen to have three homicide investigations going. What do you want?"

"I don't want anything. I just thought you'd like to know. There's every indication that yesterday afternoon your son-in-law hired this detective Steerwell to spy on your daughter."

"What do you mean, every indication?"

I told MacAullif what had happened. He wasn't pleased.

"Why didn't you check this out yesterday?" he said, irritably.

"I didn't know about it yesterday."

"You knew he went into the building."

"It was a building of stockbrokers. It was logical that was where he was going."

"You can't always go by what's logical. You have to consider all possibilities."

"How? I couldn't get in the elevator with him. You didn't want him to see me."

"You should have read the whole call board."

"I thought I did."

"You thought wrong. You've been bitching to me about how nothing's happening and how bored you are. Here's the one thing that happened that you could have checked on, and you didn't do it."

I was getting pissed off. "I'm sorry," I said. I didn't sound sorry. "Perhaps you should hire a real detective, in whom you'd have more confidence. I believe I suggested that to begin with. In case you decide to, I would recommend the Minton Agency. They have the advantage of already being familiar with the case."

There was a pause.

"I'm sorry," MacAullif said. "It's personal, and I'm not thinking rationally. It's just that if I'd known about this, I could have called Barbara and warned her."

"How? What would you have said? What would you have told her? How could you have known?"

"I don't know. I told you I'm not thinking rationally. So, this guy Harold hired—this Steerwell—how long was he on the job?"

"He was there when I got there at seven-fifty this morning. He knocked off around noon."

"You sure he's not still lurking around?"

"Pretty sure. I tailed him out of town. He was heading in the direction of the address you gave me, so I assume he went home. I'll double-check, though."

"Do that. Now this morning—you're sure nothing happened?"

I hated to mislead MacAullif, but I felt I had to. And it wasn't just his being a father and my not wanting to hurt him and all that. You see, I have another serious failing as a private detective: I hate being a tattle-tale.

I didn't want to tell on Barbara.

"Nothing significant."

"That's strange," MacAullif said.

"What is?"

"If nothing happened, why would Steerwell knock off at noon? It doesn't make any sense. It only makes sense if something happened and he got what he came for."

MacAullif was back in form. And just when I didn't need him to be.

"Maybe Harold only hired him till noon."

"That doesn't make any sense."

"It might from Harold's standpoint. We don't have all the facts."

"Yeah, maybe," MacAullif said. "I should call and warn her."

"If you're gonna do that, you might as well let me ring the front doorbell and say, 'Hi, I'm the private dick hired by your father to keep an eye on you and your husband.' 'Cause if you tell her, you gotta tell her how you know. And if you can come up with a good enough reason aside from the truth, you win the Golden Turkey award."

MacAullif exhaled into the phone. "I see your point."

"So, would you like me to talk to her?"

"No."

"Then I wouldn't call her. But it's up to you. It's your daughter and your case. I'm just along for the ride."

"Yeah, yeah, I know," MacAullif said. "You're doing me a favor. I appreciate it. I'm sorry if I seem ungrateful."

"Forget it. The thing is, what do you want me to do?"

There was a pause. Then MacAullif said, "Just what you've been doing."

I refrained from dancing for joy.

"Except now you've got two jobs: keeping tabs on Harold and keeping this private dick away from my daughter."

"The latter might require personal contact."

"Don't let it."

"I may have no choice."

"All right. But call me first."

"I may not have time."

"Make time."

"That's not what I mean. I may run into a situation where I have to either let your daughter walk into a trap or warn her. It could require an instant decision. So I need yours now."

"That's bullshit," MacAullif said, irritably. "How can I answer that? It would depend on the circumstances. You say a trap. What kind of trap? How serious would the consequences be? You see what I mean?"

"I see," I said, innocently. "You're telling me to use my best judgment."

There was a long pause. "Yes, of course I am," MacAullif said. "You can't imagine how stupid this makes me feel, not being able to think straight. Yeah, use your best judgment, and let me know the minute anything breaks."

I assured MacAullif I would and hung up the phone.

Well, great, I thought. Now I have two draggy, impossible jobs instead of one. Plus I'm holding out on MacAullif, and he probably suspects it. Plus the fact that I haven't the faintest idea what I'm going to do.

Aside from that, it's going great.

I got in the car and drove out to the Dunleavy house. The station wagon was in the garage, and there was no sign of the Weasel.

I drove back to Harold's office. Some inconsiderate person had taken my parking space. I found another one a half a dozen meters down the block. I dropped the inevitable quarter in the meter, making my usual futile vow to get dimes, and walked back to the pay phone on the corner.

It was three o'clock, and I wasn't looking for any more trouble. I called Rosenberg & Stone.

It was a good thing I did. Wendy/Cheryl had a new case for me. An actual sign-up, right in Atlantic City. Wendy/Cheryl was vague on the specifics of the case, but it seemed a Floyd Watson on Connecticut Avenue had broken his leg, and some friend of his had called in and asked for a lawyer. Floyd had no phone, but he'd be home all day, and Wendy/Cheryl had assured the friend that I'd be right over.

I didn't want to go and leave Harold unguarded, but a quick look at the map showed Connecticut Avenue to be only a dozen blocks away. I figured I could zip over and sign the guy up before Harold got off work.

I got in my car and drove over. The address turned out to be on a block of row-houses in terrible repair. People were sitting out on the old wooden porches of most of them, and children were playing out front.

There was no one in front of mine, and I could see why. It was easily the worst of the lot. The front of the house was a wreck. It wasn't just a question of peeling paint, as it had been at Raymon Ortega's. Boards were coming off the wall here. The windows were nonexistent—there was nothing left, not even the frame. The door was also gone. Well, at least I'd have no problem getting in.

I went up on the little front porch. Half of it had rotted away. The remaining boards were splintered and cracked. I made my way cautiously to the door and peered in.

The hallway was full of rubbish. It was hard to believe anyone lived here. It was also hard to believe such a place existed, right under the shadow of the casinos in the city of gold.

I picked my way through the rubble to the stair. Wendy/Cheryl had said second floor. There were no lights and it was hard to see. The only light came from the front door. It was still enough to see that the stairs were a disaster. All of the steps were cracked and one of them was actually missing. There was no handrail.

Going up the stairs was an adventure. I had my briefcase, so I only had one free hand. I leaned against the side wall, and made my way up the stairs. I was careful to keep my feet near the wall, where presumably the risers were, and away from the suspicious-looking middle of the steps.

I reached the top of the stairs. There was an open door in front of me leading to a small room in the back of the house. Sunlight was streaming through the window. Just to one side, out of the glare of the light, was a mattress on the floor.

An old black man lay on the mattress, his right leg encased in a hip-length cast. His eyes were closed, and his face was contorted in pain.

"Floyd Watson?" I said.

He opened his eyes and saw me. His eyes took on some light. He actually raised up on one elbow.

"You a doctor?" he grunted.

"No," I said. "I'm from the lawyers' office."

"Aw, shit," he moaned, and sank back on the bed again.

It wasn't the most cordial greeting I've ever gotten, but I wasn't about to fault a man in pain.

"Are you all right?" I asked him.

He grimaced and shook his head. "Damn doctors won't give me no drugs," he said.

"Oh?"

"Treat me like some goddamn junkie. Won't trust me with no drugs."

"Are you in pain?" I asked, stupidly.

He looked at me. "What are you, comedian? Yeah, I'm in pain. Damn hospital throw me out, don't give me no drugs."

"When'd they release you?"

"This mornin'."

"When'd you break your leg?"

"Las' night."

I shook my head. "They shouldn't have released you that quick."

He snorted. "Hell, they want to keep me. I won't stay. Damn hospital."

"Anybody looking after you?"

"Yeah. My buddy. He out gettin' some pain killer now. He get up enough money for a pint, things look a lot better."

Despite the pain, he managed to cock his head at me and give me a sly smile.

I liked him. He was a game old codger. One of those clients you get every now and then that it gives you some satisfaction to help.

"How'd you break your leg?"

"Fell down the stairs."

I could understand that. In fact, it was a minor miracle *I* hadn't broken my leg on the stairs.

"Who owns this building?" I asked him.

He cocked his head at me. "How the hell should I know?"

"Well, who you pay the rent to?"

"Don' pay no rent."

"You live here?"

"That's right."

"How long you live here?"

"Goin' on ten years now."

"And you never paid any rent?"

"Hell, no."

I looked at him. "And no one ever bothered you?"

"Why the hell anyone bother me? Who want this piece of shit, anyhow? I live here, mind my own business, no one pay no mind. No one care about this place. Why the hell they want to hassle me?"

I felt bad. It was a great case—a serious injury and a glaring defect—tremendous liability. Except for one thing. No defendant.

It was a new one on me. Everyone knows who owns their building. Or at least they know who they pay the rent to. But Floyd Watson paid no rent. So who did we sue?

I knew it wouldn't be hard to find out. All I had to do was go to the County Clerk's office and look up the tax record for the building. But that wasn't part of the sign-up. I wasn't supposed to do that unless Richard requested it as a separate assignment. And I doubted if he would, despite the fact it only would have cost him ten or twenty bucks. I could have done it myself, just out of the goodness of my heart, and not even mentioned it, just included the info on the sign-up sheet, but I figured it wouldn't do any good. I figured Richard would reject the case.

I'm not a lawyer, so I didn't know the legal ramifications of Floyd Watson not paying rent, but I knew there'd be some. Did that technically make him a trespasser and therefore make the owner not liable? Or did his living there ten years give him squatter's rights? I didn't know.

But I did know Richard. And I knew he was a

demon in court and loved a good fight. But what he loved fighting about was the *extent* of the liability and the *amount* of the damages. He didn't want to have to argue the question of whether liability existed at all. He wanted simple, straightforward cases. Anything borderline just wasn't worth his time.

I knew he'd turn Floyd Watson down.

Still, I had to finish the sign-up. I forced a smile, and said, "So, you don't know who owns the building?"

"No, I don't," Floyd said irritably. "What difference it make, anyway?"

"Well, we have to know who to sue. The guy who owns the building is responsible for not fixing the stairs."

"Stairs?" Floyd said, frowning. "What stairs? Oh. No, no. Not them stairs. Didn't fall on them stairs."

I looked at him. "I'm sorry. I thought you said you did."

He shook his head. "Not them stairs."

"Oh? Well, what stairs did you fall on?"

He grimaced as a spasm of pain hit him again. It passed, and his eyes opened again. He looked at me and jerked his thumb over his shoulder. "In the casino," he said.

I loved it.

11

Harold came out of his office building at five o'clock on the dot, went to the parking lot, and picked up his car. I was already in my car, all fired up and ready to go. But Harold foxed me. Instead of heading back toward Absecon, he went the other way.

I was not familiar with all the traffic regulations in Atlantic City, but I would have been willing to bet you U-turns on Atlantic Avenue were among the prohibited. I made one anyway, and caught up with Harold in less than three blocks.

It was a good thing I did, because a few blocks further Harold hung a left. I hung one too and tagged along, hoping like hell this time he was heading for the Boardwalk and the casinos.

He was. He pulled into the parking garage of Tallman's, the newest casino on the Boardwalk. If there was any question as to its being the newest, it was settled by huge banners over the doors. "GRAND OPENING," "BIGGEST SLOT PAYOFF IN TOWN," and "UNLIMITED FREE PARKING," were the lures. The banners were somewhat faded and torn, indicating the grand opening was probably somewhere into its sixth month or so, but who was I to quibble. It was still pretty new.

I followed Harold around and around until we spiraled up to the fifth level where he found a parking place. I found one a dozen cars down. I got out, locked my car and saw that Harold was heading in the direction of the elevator on the far wall. I headed for it, too.

There were half a dozen people waiting for the elevator. It came, and I had a decision to make. Did I get in the elevator with Harold and risk him getting a good look at me, or did I attract even more attention to myself by standing there like an asshole while the doors closed in my face?

I opted for the elevator. I'm sure it was a good choice. Harold seemed preoccupied. He never even glanced in my direction.

The elevator arrived at the ground floor and we got out. I followed a few steps behind as Harold walked down the hall and into the casino.

Harold and I wove our way through the maze of slot machines to the middle of the room, where the real games were.

The gamblers at the tables were being brought drinks by girls with skimpy costumes designed so that their breasts were pushed up to an incredible height and jiggled like jello and seemed perpetually on the brink of jumping out. I wondered if Harold had something going with one of them. It seemed likely. It would explain why Harold had driven to this casino, when there were others closer to his office.

Harold ignored the girls, however, and made his way down the line to a blackjack table where three men were playing. Harold pulled out a roll of money, sat down, and bought some chips from the dealer.

The dealer was a young woman. A blonde. Her hair was pulled back from her face and tied at the back of her head. She wore just a hint of makeup. She was dressed in a simple, discreet, light blue pants suit.

She was gorgeous.

The girls with the bouncing boobs were cheap and obvious. This girl was class.

I figured I'd found Harold's outside interest.

Harold paid no attention to her, however. He concentrated on the cards. I chose an unobtrusive vantage point and watched.

It was fairly simple and straightforward. The cards were in a metal shoe. The players would place their bets. Then the woman would slide cards out of the shoe one at a time, and deal them, two up to each player, and one down and one up to herself. She then dealt cards to the players who wanted hits. Then she faced her hole card, and stood or drew, depending on whether she had seventeen or less. Then she collected the losses and paid off the wins.

I watched for hours. During that time, some players left the table, and others joined the game. Some of the men attempted to kid the attractive dealer, who remained politely aloof.

Harold was not one of them. The dealer might not have existed for him. He concentrated fiercely on his cards.

And there was a pattern to his playing.

There was a five dollar minimum at the table, and that's what Harold usually bet. Except every now and then he'd bet higher, one large bet.

There were two things in common about Harold's large bets. They always came when the dealer got near the end of the deck. And Harold always won.

That, coupled with Harold's intense concentration, led me to a conclusion.

Harold was a card counter.

The thing about my conclusions is, the minute I

reach 'em, I start to doubt 'em. This time was no exception. Harold's style of play could be explained by the fact that he was a card counter. But it didn't explain the fact that he always won. Moreover, the players made their bets before they got their cards. Counting cards might tell you whether to hit or stand on a particular hand, but it couldn't tell you what hand was likely to win before it was dealt. So you knew what cards were left in the deck—so what? Another player or the dealer could get 'em just as well as you. You couldn't count on winning.

But Harold did. And the size of his large bets kept increasing. He'd started with a couple of hundred dollars, and in the beginning his big bets had been around that. But as his stack of chips grew, he was risking more and more on his one-shot deals. The maximum bet allowed was twenty-five hundred dollars, and by the time I was working this out in my head, Harold had worked his bankroll up to that, and was betting it each time he popped for the big one.

Which wasn't often. He didn't do it on every deal through the deck. Sometimes four or five decks would go by before Harold would plunge. Before he figured the cards were right. In the hour and a half after Harold had worked up to the limit, he only managed to make two maximum bets, both of which he won.

A half an hour later he bet the max again.

And he lost.

I was in position to see his face when it happened. I was glad I was. So many expressions registered on that face.

He looked furious. He looked incredulous. He looked disappointed. He looked shocked.

And one thing more.

He looked betrayed.

He made one more big bet after that. That one he

won. When he did, he looked at his watch, so I looked at mine. It was 10:45. Harold gathered up his chips, went to the cashier's window, and cashed out.

I figured he was up close to seventy-five hundred dollars.

If having that much cash on him bothered Harold, he didn't show it. He just shoved the bills in his pocket and headed for the elevator.

Luckily, there were two elevators loading on the ground floor, so I didn't have to get in the one with him. Mine reached the fifth level first. I got out and went straight to my car. As I gunned the motor, I could see Harold getting into his. I let him pull out first, then followed him down the spiral ramp.

Harold drove back to Atlantic Avenue, turned onto it, and pulled in at a meter. I had to go on by. I pulled into a meter halfway down the block. I got out and started walking back. I had a flash of panic. Harold was nowhere in sight. Then I spotted him. He was still sitting in his car.

I walked on by to the corner. Then I stopped and made a show of snapping my fingers angrily, as if I'd forgotten something, just in case Harold was watching. Then I turned around and walked back to my car.

I hopped in my car, pulled out, turned right, back toward the Boardwalk, went one block, turned right again, went two blocks, discovered the street I wanted was one-way, went one more block, turned right, sped up to Atlantic Avenue hoping I hadn't blown it, turned right on Atlantic, slowed down, and crept up on where Harold had parked his car.

He was still there. I spotted his car from a block away. I pulled into the curb about a half a block behind him, switched off the lights and killed the motor.

We waited.

She was out by 11:15. She came around the corner,

stepping right along, her blonde hair loose and flowing in the breeze. She must have got off at eleven and taken time to change. I was glad she had. I must say, the shorts and tank top showed her figure to much better advantage than her dealer's uniform. She was a dish.

She hopped in the car and Harold pulled out.

I followed them to a small apartment building in Linwood. Harold parked in front of the building. He and the girl got out and went in.

I watched from across the street. A couple of minutes later a light went on in the second floor window.

I got out of my car, crossed the street, and went in. It was a small foyer with a row of mail slots and bells. I pushed on the inner door. It was unlocked. I went in and up the stairs.

The door to the front apartment was number 2A. I didn't knock on it. I went back to the foyer and looked at the mailboxes. 2A was listed as "M. Carson."

I went back and sat in my car.

About two o'clock Harold came out, got in his car and drove off.

I followed him home.

The house was dark. Harold put the car in the garage, locked it and went in the front door. He did not turn on the light.

I sat in my car.

O.K. I had the picture now. Harold had found a greener pasture and a financial bonanza to boot. He was set on trading in his old-model wife on her, and he didn't want to go broke paying alimony, so he'd hired the Weasel to dig up some dirt.

Yeah, that was the picture all right. But it was your basic, sordid little *domestic* picture. MacAullif had said Harold was in trouble. I could think of a lot of guys who would have loved to have Harold's problems.

So either MacAullif was wrong, or I didn't have the whole picture yet.

I realized one thing sitting in my car. It didn't matter whether MacAullif was right or wrong. The point was, I had held out on him, and by doing so I had put his daughter in jeopardy. I had taken the responsibility on myself.

It was up to me to do something about it.

12

I got up at six A.M., showered, shaved, put on my suit and tie, drove in to Atlantic City, took out my camera and shot every crack in the sidewalk I could find. I had six rolls of film in my briefcase. I shot 'em all.

By nine o'clock, I was all finished and sitting in my car when a pudgy girl carrying a paper bag came down the street and unlocked the Photomat. She was still turning on the lights when I walked in and set my six rolls of film on the counter.

The girl looked at me, and then somewhat ruefully at the paper bag, which I assumed contained coffee and doughnuts, probably jelly. She gave me what I considered to be a somewhat insincere smile, reached under the counter, took out a stack of film envelopes, and counted out six of them. She folded the envelope flap receipts over, tore them off, and stapled them together. She picked up a pen.

"Name?"

"Minton Agency."

She nodded, scrawled "Minton" on the top envelope, and set the envelopes and the six rolls aside. She handed me the six receipts.

"You got anything going back?" I asked her.

She had. Thirteen rolls. She gave 'em to me, too, no sweat. I'd figured she would. I have a friend, Fred Lazar, who runs a detective agency in Manhattan, so I knew how the system works. All the operatives come in and drop off their film all day long, and the one that's heading for the office picks everything up. They never bother with the receipts. They just ask for the pix for the agency. I'd picked up film for Fred Lazar a couple of times myself. So I figured if it worked in Manhattan it would work here.

It worked like a charm. I didn't even have to pay. I signed the name Robert Fuller in the account book.

Pudgy didn't care. She was thinking about her doughnuts. She was already diving for the bag as I went out the door.

I got in the car and drove back to the hotel. Maybe I'm just paranoid, but somehow I didn't want to be sitting looking at these pictures in the car.

I double-locked the door, since the maid hadn't been there to make up the room yet. I went to the table, dumped the packets of film out of the plastic bag, and started going through them.

It took a while, what with there being thirteen rolls. Of course, most of them meant nothing to me. The first few rolls I examined featured businessmen in suits and ties, usually two of 'em talking together. They obviously didn't know they were being photographed. That figured. Somehow I couldn't figure the Weasel going, "Say cheese."

One man featured prominently in several rolls. I dubbed him the King. He was a stout, middle-aged man, with dark hair, gray at the temples, and an aristocratic bearing. He wore a gold chain with a gold medallion around his neck. His face was plump and his skin was smooth like a baby's, but his eyes were hard.

The only other man who stood out was the one I dubbed the Bear. He was only on one roll, and the only reason I noticed him was because he was so ugly. He was a fat man, with dark, bushy hair and thick, dark stubble—not a beard—just stubble. He looked like something you wouldn't want to meet on a camping trip.

The eighth roll was the one I wanted.

The pictures were not good. They'd been shot through the gap in the drapes, so the curtains had cut off an inch on either side of the shot. But the middle was all too clear.

I looked at the picture in my hands, shook my head, and let out a sigh.

Barbara MacAullif Dunleavy was sitting on the bed with her head and shoulders propped up on the pillows. Her tank top was still on. But her shorts and panties were not. Her knees were drawn up and her legs were spread wide. The tree surgeon, naked as a jay bird, was kneeling between them, performing cunnilingus.

I thought of MacAullif. I thought about calling him now. "Yeah, I got something. I got some shots of your daughter getting her pussy licked."

Poor Barbara. Done in by a half-inch gap in the curtain. She'd remembered to pull the drapes, but had forgotten to make sure they crossed.

Absurdly, lines from Wordsworth sprang to mind. "Not in utter nakedness, and not in entire forgetfulness" seemed rather apt. "Trailing clouds of glory" was a bit of a stretch, however.

I looked through the rest of the shots. Some were better than others, but all of them were essentially the same.

I put the pictures back in the envelope, marked it

with an X so I could tell it from the others, and looked at the rest of the rolls. None of the others were Barbara.

I put the packets of photos in the plastic bag, and shoved it into my suitcase.

All right, I thought, what the fuck do I do now? I mean, I'd retrieved the photographs, that was good, but the threat of the Weasel still remained, and I still wasn't any closer to the root of Harold's problems.

I got in the car and drove over to the Dunleavy house. There was no sign of the Weasel. The station wagon was also gone, so Barbara was out. What I didn't know, of course, was whether the Weasel was following her.

I had to do something. After all, if the Weasel got some more photographs, all the good I'd accomplished would go right down the drain.

MacAullif didn't want me talking to Barbara or Harold, but he hadn't said anything about talking to the Weasel.

I drove back to Atlantic City, parked my car, and went up to the Minton Agency. The antisocial secretary was still typing a letter. I wondered if it was the same one.

This time I didn't bother waiting for her to glance up. "Joe Steerwell," I said.

She didn't glance up then.

"Not in yet," she grunted, and went on typing.

I got back in my car and drove out to the Weasel's house. It was a two-story affair out in Margate. I went up on the front porch and rang the bell.

There was no answer. I hadn't expected any. The blue Chevy wasn't parked in the driveway. I rang the bell a few more times just to be sure.

As I was coming down off the front porch, a fortyish woman with teased red hair and too much lipstick came out on the porch next door.

"You looking for Joey?" she called.

"Yes," I said. "You seen him?"

"He's not home."

I could have guessed that. But I smiled anyway, as if she had imparted some useful information.

"Oh," I said.

"Yes, he went out early this morning."

"Any idea when he'll be back?"

"Could be any time now. That's the way he is. In and out, in and out, all day long."

"I'll try back later," I said.

"I'll tell him you were here," she said.

I knew she was going to say that. She was a busy-body, the type of nosy biddy that makes my blood boil. She was trying to find out my name.

I didn't give it to her. I smiled, nodded, said, "Thanks" and hopped in the car and drove off, leaving her disappointed.

I figured I was doing good works and all, as for as MacAullif was concerned, and had he known he'd have no reason to complain. But seeing as how it was getting on toward noon, I figured it was time for me to obey the prime directive.

I drove to Harold's office, parked the car, and put a quarter in the meter. I stood and watched the front door.

Some fun. Right, MacAullif. Ninety percent of sur-veillance is just hanging around. They also serve who only stand and wait.

Harold came out at 12:30, and this time he came out alone. He also went in the opposite direction that he usually went for lunch. I stuck a quarter in the meter and tagged along behind.

Harold went down Atlantic Avenue a few blocks and turned on St. Charles. He went into an office building. This time I hit the lobby just as the elevator door closed. I was in time to see there was no one else in it. The elevator indicator stopped on three.

Next to the elevator was a stairs. I sprinted up them, and pushed the door open a crack, just in time to see Harold walk down the hall and into an office.

He was out in five minutes.

I had a moment of panic when I thought he was headed for the stairs, but he rang the elevator instead. I ran down the stairs and was waiting across the street when he came out.

He went back past his office building to the restaurant where he'd gone the day before.

I left him there having lunch and walked back to the building I'd tailed him to. This time I took the elevator. No reason to wear myself out.

I walked down the hallway to the door where I'd seen Harold go in. On it was emblazoned, "FREDERICK NUBAR, INVESTMENT COUNSELOR."

I went through the door and found myself in a small waiting room. Two men were sitting in chairs reading magazines. A young secretary was sitting at a desk. Behind her was a closed door.

"May I help you?" she said.

"Yeah, I'd like to see Mr. Nubar," I said.

"Do you have an appointment?"

"No, but I'd like to make one."

"Then you'll have to wait. These gentlemen have appointments."

"That's fine," I told her.

"May I have your name?"

"Phil Collins."

She gave me a look, then smiled and wrote it down.

I'd already sat down and picked up a magazine before it dawned on me I'd given her the name of a rock singer.

I was halfway through my second issue of *People*

magazine when the door behind the desk opened and a man in a suit came out. He went on out the front door. A moment later another man appeared in the doorway of the inner office, and stood there talking to the secretary.

It was the Bear.

I waited until he'd gone back into his office and one of the men who was waiting had been ushered in, before I got up, smiled at the secretary and said, "I don't think I can wait, after all. I'll be back."

I got to my car just in time to see Harold return from lunch and go into his office, and just in time to realize I hadn't called Rosenberg & Stone.

I did, and went through the usual bullshit. Richard was out to lunch, but Wendy and Cheryl got on extensions and gangbanged me. It was too bad. Richard would have been mollified by learning that Floyd Watson fell in the casino, but Wendy and Cheryl couldn't have cared less. They gave me another picture assignment, tremendously urgent I was sure, and I finally got off the phone.

When my ears stopped ringing, I got in my car, turned on the air-conditioning, and gave some thought to my problem.

I needed to find out about Frederick Nubar. But I didn't know how to do it. Tailing him was no good. That's what I would have done if I hadn't known his name. I'd have followed him to his address, looked it up, and found out who he was. But I knew his name. And I knew what he did: he was an investment counselor. I knew who he was, but I didn't know who he *was,* that was the thing.

There was one way to find out. I could go back, masquerade as Phil Collins, and keep my bogus appointment. But that would be risky as hell. Investment counselor. What the hell was an investment counselor? What could I say to him? Why was I there?

I didn't know.

I thought about it some more, and finally it came to me. There was only one thing to do. And it was something I'd never done before, and something I'd never dreamed of doing in a million years. But it seemed the only thing to do, so I did it.

I hired a private detective.

13

"My rates are two hundred bucks a day, plus expenses."

I wished mine were. Jesus Christ.

His name was Mike Sallingsworth. He ran the Sallingsworth Detective Agency. I'd picked it out of a phone book. I didn't know if it was a good firm. As far as I was concerned, it had one basic thing going for it.

It wasn't Minton's.

Mike was about seventy. He had a thin face with a shock of white hair perched on the top. It gave him a somewhat whimsical look. He was wearing a light cord suit that looked old and faded, and a thin tie of the same vintage. His jacket was open and I could see the strap of his shoulder holster. I wondered when the last time was he'd pulled his gun. Or whether he was still waiting for his first.

I also wondered how much work there was for an emaciated, seventy-year-old gumshoe in Atlantic City.

"That's too high," I said.

He shrugged. "Those are our rates. Take it or leave it."

I wondered what he meant by "our." It was a small, one-room office, and he seemed to be the only one in it. I assumed it was the equivalent of the editorial "we"—the investigative "our."

I pulled out my I.D. and laid it on his desk.

"Look," I said. "I'm a visiting fireman from the City, and I need a little help. I need some information. If you can get it for me, fine, but I can't spring for any two hundred dollars. I can't write this off on expenses. It's coming out of my own pocket."

"Why?"

"I haven't been retained in this case. I'm doing it as a favor."

He stared at me. "You're down here from New York on a case with no retainer?"

"That's right."

"You out of your mind?"

"Yes. But that doesn't affect our relationship. If you can get the information, I'm willing to pay for it. But none of this two-hundred-dollars-a-day shit. I can go fifty bucks, tops."

He looked at me. Chuckled. Shook his head. "What is it you need to know?"

"Frederick Nubar," I told him.

"No shit."

"None. I need to know about Nubar. All I know is he's an investment counselor."

He chuckled again. Thought for a moment. Grinned. "O.K.," he said. "Twenty bucks."

I took a twenty out and laid it on his desk. He picked it up, folded it, and stuck it in his pocket.

He cocked his head at me. "Investment counselor is a euphemism," he said. "For your information, Frederick Nubar is a loan shark."

"Loan shark?"

"Yeah," he said. "The worst kind of loan shark. The kind that breaks heads."

14

I went out, sat in my car and thought things over. I had the picture now. Harold Dunleavy had gambled and got in over his head. Then he'd gone to a loan shark and borrowed God knows how much money to cover his debts. He couldn't meet the payments and was in serious danger of bodily harm. He'd fallen in with a crooked blackjack dealer who was helping him milk money out of the casino to pay off the Bear. The blackjack dealer was attractive enough that Harold was set on dumping his wife and kid for her and had hired a detective for that purpose. Meanwhile, his wife, abandoned and bored, had taken up playing doctor with a tree surgeon.

My task, should I choose to accept it, was to get the loan shark off Harold's back, set Harold on the straight and narrow, extricate him from the clutches of the blackjack dealer and reconcile him with his wife, after first ridding her of the attentions of the tree surgeon, at the same time forestalling the private detective and preventing him from reaching Harold's ears with reports of his wife's transgressions.

It was a task, I felt, that called for the wisdom of a Solomon. I didn't feel I had the wisdom of a Solomon. At the moment, I felt I had the wisdom of a game show host.

I went to a pay phone and called MacAullif.

"Harold's in hock to a loan shark."

"What?"

"That seems to be the root of your son-in-law's problems. He's in deep with a loan shark, an ugly fucker named Frederick Nubar with a reputation for breaking heads."

"You sure of that?"

"No, it's just surmise. But it stands to reason. I tailed Harold to Nubar's office. I wouldn't imagine it was just a social call."

"Shit."

"Yes. There's every indication this afternoon Harold paid Nubar off to the tune of anywhere up to seventy-five hundred dollars. And from the way Harold's acting, that would appear to be just a drop in the bucket."

"You're kidding. Where the hell would Harold get seventy-five hundred bucks?"

"Cheating at blackjack."

"What!?"

"Harold's in collusion with a blackjack dealer at one of the casinos. He put in four and a half hours at the table last night. He made seventy-five hundred. From the way he's acting, he must be pretty desperate. He's concentrating as if his life depended on it, which it may. The dealer's cheating for him."

"You can't cheat at blackjack. The cards come out of a shoe."

"Yeah, but they get shuffled before they get put in the shoe. The dealer's stacking the deck somehow. Harold sits there concentrating like a Buddhist monk until the cards get down near the end of the deck. Then if they're lying right, he bets the big one."

"What makes you think he's in deep?"

"Because he started last night with virtually no stake money and had to build up gradually."

"So?"

"If he were doing it for fun and games, he'd hold out enough stake money to play the next day. Apparently he's in so deep to this loan shark, he's forking over every cent he gets."

"Why wouldn't he hold out on him?"

"Nubar isn't the type of guy you hold out on. Maybe he's got a spy in the casino telling him how much Harold's knocking down. Or maybe Harold's just too scared to think straight. I don't know."

"Wait a minute. Wouldn't Harold be splitting the take with the blackjack dealer?"

"Not necessarily."

"Why not?"

"Because the blackjack dealer's a cute little blonde number that's apparently Harold's current outside interest. I tailed him back to her place last night."

MacAullif sounded skeptical. "They left together?"

"No. Harold got his car out of the garage and parked two blocks away. She showed up twenty minutes later, hopped in the car, and they took off for fun and frolic."

There was a pause. I could almost hear MacAullif thinking all that over.

"Now," I said. "You told me to find out what was going on and report to you, and then we'd figure out what to do about it. All right, I've reported."

Another pause. "Right."

"So what do you want to do?"

"Well, we have to keep Harold from getting his head broken."

"I'm not a bodyguard."

"I never said you were."

"That's less than helpful."

"I know, I know," MacAullif said. "Jesus. All right. What about the private dick Harold hired?"

"What *about* him?"

"He still on the job?"

"He wasn't when I checked this morning. That's the best I can tell you. I've been rather busy."

"So I see."

There was another pause.

"So what do you want to do?" I said. I had the feeling of having said it before.

"All right, look," MacAullif said. "This thing about Harold and the loan shark—I gotta think about it. At the moment it seems to be status quo. Harold's just made a payment, that should hold the guy at least twenty-four hours, anyway.

"But this private dick he hired is another thing. We can't let him give Harold any hard evidence on my daughter. Harold's a slime and a shit, and he'd use it."

"No argument there."

"So that's your main concern for the moment. Keep tabs on the dick and let me know if he makes a move on my daughter."

"That's a roundabout and highly ineffective way of doing it. The only way to be sure is for me to talk to your daughter."

"No. Absolutely not."

"I can make up a story. She doesn't have to know who I am."

"No, no. It wouldn't work. Barbara's too sharp. You do it just the way I tell you. You don't keep her away from Steerwell. You keep Steerwell away from her."

"But—"

"Look, I got three murders on my hands here. I gotta go. You're doing fine. Just play it the way I said."

He hung up the phone.

I must admit I slammed the receiver down.

Hell!

Doing fine, was I? Well, it was sure nice of him to let me know.

I thought about it some and decided, hell, if that's the way MacAullif wanted me to play it, that's how I'd play it.

Wonderful. Around and around Atlantic City, the private dick chased the Weasel.

It was three o'clock, so I checked in with Rosenberg & Stone and then drove out to Margate City. I must say I wasn't happy. Aside from everything else, MacAullif had seemed strangely reticent on the phone. It wasn't like him. Even in this case, and even though it was family. He'd seemed confused before and not quite himself, but not reticent.

I didn't like it.

On Ventnor Avenue a car passed me going back the other way that looked a lot like Harold's, and I realized I'd left him alone since after lunch. I wondered if it was really him. I wasn't about to turn around and find out, however. I kept going to the Weasel's house.

This time his car was parked in the driveway. But I didn't stop. I drove on by and parked a couple of houses down the street.

Because another car was parked in front of the Weasel's house. A Chevy station wagon. One I thought I knew.

I got out of my car. As I did, I heard a bloodcurdling scream. It came from the direction of the Weasel's house.

Barbara MacAullif Dunleavy came running out the front door. She was screaming hysterically. She stopped on the front porch and looked around, frantically. She had a gun in her hand. She seemed to see it for the first time. She looked at it, screamed, and threw it on the ground.

FAVOR

Miss Busybody from next door came out on her porch. Barbara saw her, screamed again, ran to the station wagon, jumped in and drove off.

I jumped in my car and gave chase. I probably would have caught her, but just my luck, I got stopped by a cop. How he let her go by and stopped me is beyond me, but the guy did. He gave me a speeding ticket, too.

It occurred to me it wasn't my day. It also occurred to me not many of them were.

It also occurred to me Barbara MacAullif Dunleavy was in deep shit. I figured I'd better find out how deep.

I turned around and drove back to the Weasel's house.

I didn't turn into his street. I didn't have to. Just driving by I could see a half a dozen police cars with flashing lights on top and a meat wagon parked out front.

Deep shit, indeed.

Pop goes the Weasel.

15

I didn't call Rosenberg & Stone at five o'clock. Frankly, I didn't even think of it. I had other things on my mind and other things to do.

I was halfway out to the Dunleavy's when I remembered the pictures. What a jerk. I'd forgotten all about them. The Weasel was dead, and I had his pictures. So far nobody knew that, but it was a murder investigation now, and with all my errands for MacAullif, I couldn't count on keeping myself in the dark for long.

I drove back downtown to the post office and bought a mailer. I went back to the hotel, got the bag of pictures out of my suitcase and packed them in it. I addressed it to myself, General Delivery, Atlantic City. I figured I wanted them out of the way, but where I could put my hands on them if I had to. I drove around, found a mailbox, and dropped the package in.

That was at five o'clock, the time I should have called Rosenberg & Stone. I didn't think of it because to me, five o'clock meant just one thing.

The local news would be on.

I switched on the car radio and found a local station.

It was the lead story. "Murder in Margate," said the newscaster. He went on to give out all the details they had on the demise of Joseph T. Steerwell. There were a lot. He'd been shot in the face with a .38-caliber automatic. The gun had been recovered at the scene of the crime. It had been carried from the house and dropped on the front lawn by a young woman who had escaped in a station wagon. The woman was described as in her midtwenties, short black hair, medium height and build, attractive. I figured the "attractive" had come grudgingly from Miss Busybody.

The woman was not the only suspect however. There was also a young man who had entered the house some ten minutes before. He had been observed by the next door neighbor, one Priscilla Martin, entering and leaving the house. He had been inside for less than five minutes. He had seemed terribly agitated when he left. The man was described as in his midthirties, 5'10" to 6 feet, 165 pounds, dark hair and blue eyes, wearing a suit and tie.

Leave it to Miss Busybody, I thought. She'd described Barbara and Harold Dunleavy to a T.

The news report concluded with speculation as to whether the man had shot the victim and the woman had merely found the gun and picked it up, or whether the woman had brought the gun and shot him.

It was an incredibly detailed report. I couldn't imagine the police giving out that many facts. I figured they probably hadn't. They probably just had been unable to stifle Miss Busybody.

One thing puzzled me about the story. There was no mention of a shot. Surely Miss Busybody must have heard one. And if she had heard a shot while either Harold or Barbara was in the Weasel's house, that would have clinched the case. So why hadn't she mentioned it? Or, if she had, why wasn't it part of the story?

I tried to think back to when I'd seen Barbara running from the house. It had all happened so fast that it was blurred in my memory. But it seemed to me the gun she was carrying had a long barrel.

I wondered if it had a silencer.

One other thing puzzled me about the story. Why the hell would Harold have wanted to kill the Weasel? He'd hired him, for Christ's sake. Barbara might have wanted to, but not Harold.

Unless.

I remembered the pictures I'd looked at that morning, the pictures I'd mailed to myself.

The pictures of the Bear.

As so often seems to happen to me in the course of my life, I felt like a total asshole. What a shmuck! Anyone with half a brain would have looked at the pictures before putting them in the mailer. I mean, Jesus Christ. The Weasel had taken pictures of the Bear. The Bear was a notorious loan shark with a reputation for breaking heads. The Weasel's head had been broken. It didn't take an Einstein to know that those pictures might be important.

But I hadn't looked at them.

Some detective.

Sallingsworth had given me the Bear's address. It was out in Somers Point.

I drove out there. I went by the Weasel's on the way. I thought of stopping in to chat with Miss Busybody. I decided against it. She was a loudmouth and she was cooperating with the police. I didn't want her telling them about me.

There were lights on in the Bear's house and there was a car in the drive.

I went up on the front porch and rang the bell.

I must confess, I didn't know what I was going to say. I hadn't stopped to think about it. If I had, I wouldn't have been there. I was winging it. I was doing it quickly and impulsively, which was the only way I could have done it. As I've said, I'm not long on guts, and calling on a scary Bear who has people hurt is not my idea of a good time.

But I had to do something. The Weasel was dead, the Bear was my only other lead, so here I was.

Grasping at straws.

There was no answer. That was strange, what with the car there and the lights on.

I peered in the front window. The drapes were pulled, but as with Barbara's, there was a small gap. Through the gap, I could see the end of a couch and a coffee table.

Near the end of the coffee table was a shoe. There was nothing particularly strange in that. I often sit on the couch, take off my shoes, and leave 'em lying under the coffee table.

Only the toe of this one was pointing up.

I tried the front door. It was unlocked. I pushed it open and went in. I went through the foyer and into the living room.

There was a man lying on the floor. It was the Bear. He'd been shot once in the face.

The Bear was dead as a mackerel.

16

The Bear was only the second dead body I'd ever seen. The first one had been stabbed in the back with a knife. There'd been a lot of blood, but his face hadn't been messed up. The Bear'd been shot right in the bridge of the nose, which had splintered. Blood covered most of his face. I can't say it marred his appearance, though. In his case, it was almost an improvement.

None of those thoughts ran through my mind when I found the body. The only thing that occurred to me was that I was going to be sick. I ran out the front door and heaved my guts out over the rail of the front porch.

I'd thrown up when I'd found my first body, too. So at least I'm consistent.

When I'd recovered some of my composure, I looked around to see if anyone had been watching my performance. No one had. I took a deep breath, which forced some particularly nauseating air into my nose and mouth, and blew it out again. All right. So what did I do now?

I knew the first thing I had to do. I had to go back inside and look at the body again, and see what I could deduce from it. See if I could find any clues.

I didn't want to do it. I didn't figure I'd necessarily throw up again, but on the other hand, when I write down my Christmas wishes, looking at bloody dead bodies is not high on the list.

You can't always get what you want. I went back inside and looked at the body. It was easier the second time. Still not fun, but easier. At least I managed to stay in the room.

I walked all around the body, observed it from every angle. I studied its position in the room. After careful analysis, my expert opinion was this: someone who didn't like the Bear had shot him in the face.

I went through his pockets. It took me a bit to persuade myself to do this, but not much. Barbara and Harold were in pretty deep. And I was getting in pretty deep myself.

I found nothing interesting. The most I learned was the body hadn't been robbed. The Bear had three hundred and some odd dollars in his wallet. I'd never robbed a corpse before, and I wasn't about to start now. I left it there.

The wallet had the usual number of credit cards, a driver's license, and a Blue Cross/Blue Shield card. Pretty small pickings, except for the three hundred bucks.

The other pockets were even less rewarding. Some pens, some small change, a handkerchief, and some keys on a ring. No notebook with names and addresses. No letters.

Not a clue.

I stood up and looked at the body again. The Bear hadn't done anything helpful, like scrawling the name of his killer in blood on the floor. He'd just fallen over backwards and expired.

O.K. So what did I do now?

The first time I'd found a dead body I'd called the

police and waited for them to arrive. I didn't want to get in a rut. I got the hell out of there.

I drove back to Atlantic City, stopped at a pay phone and called the police. They put me on hold. I waited about two minutes, then a bored-sounding voice came on the line.

"Yeah?" it said.

"I want to report a homicide."

"What?"

"A homicide. I'm reporting a homicide." I gave the guy the address of the Bear's house.

He seemed a little less bored. "Who are you?" he asked.

I hung up and drove out to the Dunleavy house. Lights were on and the station wagon was in the garage.

The convertible was gone.

I drove back to Atlantic City and parked in Tallman's garage. I went into the casino.

Harold was sitting at the blackjack table. The blonde, presumably M. Carson, was dealing. Harold was concentrating on his cards, same as always.

I had to admire Harold, somehow. Admire his cool. If Miss Busybody were to be believed, Harold at best had found the Weasel's body and knew he was dead, and at worst had killed him. And yet, here he was, playing cards as if nothing had happened.

I wondered if Harold knew that his obligation to the Bear was over. I wondered if he'd be playing cards so intently if he knew he didn't need the money so desperately.

On the other hand, if Harold could be so cool about the Weasel, maybe he could be that cool about the Bear, too. I wondered if he was.

I wondered if Harold had killed the Bear.

While I was wondering that, a group of men made

their way through the center of the room. That probably sounds strange—after all, lots of men were wandering all around the huge room. But this group was different. They moved en masse, like a procession, somehow. Like a retinue.

The man in the center was clearly in charge, was clearly the big cheese. His tailor-made suit looked like a million bucks.

The men stopped right in front of me, so I could get a good look at them. One of the men was talking animatedly to the big cheese, but I could tell he wasn't listening. His attention seemed to be on the blackjack table, where the blonde was dealing the cards. The big cheese seemed pretty interested in the blonde.

Even without his gold chain and medallion, I could recognize the big cheese.

He was the King.

It was a little much. I mean, come on, give me a break. This was getting to be like one of those fucking Ross Mcdonald novels where everyone is involved with everyone else and the plot keeps turning back in on itself. Not that they're not damn good, by the way. I just didn't want to *live* one.

This morning I'd looked at pictures taken by the Weasel. Among them were shots of the Bear and the King. Since then, the Weasel had been shot in the face. The Bear had been shot in the face. And here was the King, presumably the owner of Tallman's Casino, standing and looking at the blonde dealing blackjack to Harold Dunleavy and presumably cheating to boot so that Harold Dunleavy would have enough money to pay off the Bear. And Harold Dunleavy had hired the Weasel to spy on his wife.

All right. Next case.

The King and his retinue moved on.

I moved on, too. I didn't need to watch Harold and

the girl work the blackjack scam. I'd seen that routine. I got my car and drove off.

I didn't feel like driving all the way out to Somers Point to see if the police had taken my phone call seriously. Fortunately I didn't have to. It was on the local news. I don't know how the reporters get on to those things—some cop must tip 'em off—but they were damn good.

Frederick Nubar had been found shot dead in his Somers Point home. He'd been shot once in the face. There were no suspects and no motive for the murder. It was not yet known if there was any connection between this murder and the murder of Joseph T. Steerwell of Margate, who had also been discovered shot in the face in his home earlier in the day.

I could have called the reporter up and suggested a connection. I didn't do it. I sat in my car and tried to think what to do next.

I still hadn't called MacAullif. And I wasn't about to. You see, Barbara MacAullif had gone to see the Weasel. Whether she shot him or not, she'd been out there. And there were only two people that knew that Harold had hired the Weasel to spy on his wife: MacAullif and me. And I sure hadn't told her.

Which meant MacAullif had. It was the only explanation. After agonizing about it, he'd called her and warned her. And if he had, as I'd pointed out to him, he'd have had to tell her how he knew. There'd be no other way out.

That was why MacAullif had sounded so reticent on the phone. No wonder he didn't want me to warn her. He'd *already* warned her. After forbidding me to do it, he'd gone ahead and done it himself. And he was so embarrassed about it, he couldn't bring himself to tell me.

I can't say that I blamed him. It was his daughter. It

was family. Blood is thicker than water. But the thing was, he'd warned her. And the thing was, that was *before* anything had happened. That was when her biggest trouble was some private dick snooping around. Now it was a double homicide. And MacAullif's daughter was mixed up in it right up to her eyebrows. He'd move heaven and earth to save her. He'd do anything. Whatever else might happen, he'd save her first. So I couldn't really count on his support anymore.

I was on my own.

I wondered if I should wait and tail Harold when he left the casino. I wondered if I should say, "Fuck MacAullif," and drive over and have a little talk with Barbara.

I realized I didn't feel like doing either. It had been a hell of a day, both physically and emotionally. I was exhausted, and I needed some sleep. I drove back to the hotel.

The cops were there waiting for me.

17

There were two of 'em. They were waiting in my hotel room. I just walked in and there they were.

They were in plain clothes, so they didn't necessarily have to be cops. They also could have been hit men. In fact, my first thought when I walked in was that I was about to get a bullet in the face. So it was actually a relief when they turned out to be cops.

But not much.

I'd never walked into a hotel room and found cops waiting for me before. TV detectives do it all the time. They're used to it, and it doesn't faze them in the least. And they always have some snappy, sardonic one-liner ready, such as, "Don't mind me, gentlemen, just make yourselves right at home." That would have been appropriate now, since the taller of the two, all six-foot-four of him, was stretched out on the bed, and the shorter, stockier one with the dark moustache was sitting at the table reading a newspaper. However, I wasn't quite up to any snappy one-liners. The best I could manage was to stand there looking stupid.

Fortunately they took the initiative. The tall one sat up and swung his legs over the side of the bed. The one with the moustache folded his paper, stood up, and said, "Stanley Hastings?"

I had a wild impulse to say, "No, room service," and duck back out the door. It was momentary, however. I gulped. "Yes."

Moustache reached in his jacket pocket, and flopped open his badge. "Lieutenant Barnes." He pointed to the guy on the bed. "This is Sergeant Preston."

Despite myself, I blurted, "You're kidding."

The sergeant grinned, which almost relaxed me for a moment. "I get that all the time," he said.

"What can I do for you gentlemen?" I said. I was pleased with myself. That sounded more like what a TV detective would say.

Lieutenant Barnes smiled. "We were hoping you could assist us with our inquiries."

I felt a chill. I read British detective fiction, so I knew that phrase was a euphemism the police gave out to the press to describe someone they were holding on suspicion of murder. I wondered if Barnes read British detective fiction, too.

"What inquiries?"

"Forgive me," Barnes said. "We're with Major Crimes. We handle all serious felonies, particularly murder. In this case we have two. The murder of Joseph T. Steerwell, and the murder of Frederick Nubar. A pair of rather puzzling crimes. We were hoping you could shed some light on them."

My mind was reeling. How the hell had these guys gotten onto me so fast? How much were they groping in the dark, and how much did they know?

And what the hell should I do?

The smart thing, I knew, was to say nothing—"Fuck you, I'm not talking, I want to call my lawyer." But if I did that, the die would be cast. I'd be out in the open, me against them. They would probably run me in, and I'd sit in jail until something happened. And having chosen not to talk, there I'd be, helpless, sitting there like a fool, unable to defend myself or do anything else useful. And then how dumb would I feel when it turned out these guys had nothing on me anyway, and just wanted to talk.

So I decided not to tell the gentlemen to get fucked. I could always clam up later. But for the time being, I'd just play dumb and innocent.

"I'd like to help you," I said. "But I'm afraid I don't know anything about it."

Barnes fished a notebook out of his jacket pocket. "That's strange," he said, "because a Michael Sallingsworth of the Sallingsworth Detective Agency says that you were in there today trying to get information on one Frederick Nubar."

So. Sallingsworth had sold me out. I wondered if it was because I was a piker who'd only paid him twenty bucks. I realized the thought was uncharitable. Sallingsworth was a licensed private detective. He had to work in Atlantic City. And this was murder. He couldn't hold out on the cops on something like this.

Frankly, I was relieved. Of all the ways the cops could have got a line on me, this was the best. So I'd inquired about Nubar. It didn't connect me with the Weasel. It didn't lead the cops to Harold and Barbara. As far as being fucked went, it was the best of all possible worlds.

"I see," I said.

"Could you tell us the reason for your interest in Frederick Nubar?" Barnes asked.

"If you will pardon me, Lieutenant," I said, "I've had a hard day, and if this is going to take any time, I'm going to sit down."

I walked by him and sat at the table. I was stalling for time, which I was sure the Lieutenant was aware of. I also wanted to see if he would let me do it. I didn't know how they did things in Atlantic City—whether they resorted to third degrees, rubber hoses, and the like—and I thought I might get a hint.

Barnes was all courtesy. He stepped aside and let me sit. Preston came around the bed, and the two cops stood, flanking me at the table. Looking up at him from that angle made Preston seem incredibly tall.

"If you're quite comfortable," Barnes said, "perhaps you could tell us about Frederick Nubar."

"What about him?"

"What's your interest in him?"

"You know I'm a private detective?"

"That's what Sallingsworth said."

"He's an excellent source of information. That's what I am. I work for the law firm of Rosenberg & Stone."

"And where are they located?"

"In Manhattan."

Barnes nodded his head. "That's what I thought. And just what brings you to Atlantic City, Mr. Hastings?"

"I happen to be here on business."

"For Rosenberg & Stone?"

"That's right."

"A New York firm?"

"If you check, you'll find Richard Rosenberg is licensed to practice in New Jersey. I handle many Jersey cases."

"What kind of cases?"

"Litigation."

"Litigation? You mean civil suits?"

"Accident cases, mostly."

His face showed comprehension. "Oh. You're an ambulance chaser."

I winced, and put on a mock-deprecating look. "I prefer the term 'scum-sucking pig.' "

Preston frowned, but Barnes actually grinned.

"You do trip-and-falls, broken arms and legs?"

"That's right."

"I see. And what particular case brings you to Atlantic City?"

I rubbed my head. "Well," I said. "I don't know if my employer would be too pleased about me talking about his business. But I guess it can't hurt to tell you. I happen to be investigating the case of one Floyd Watson, of Connecticut Avenue, who fell down a flight of stairs and broke his leg."

Barnes and Preston looked at each other. Barnes looked back at me.

"You expect us to believe you came all the way down here from New York just because some guy fell down the stairs?"

I grinned at him. "You would if I told you what stairs."

Barnes thought that over. "In a casino?"

I grinned.

Barnes frowned. "All right. Then how does Nubar come into it?"

I shook my head. "I'm sorry. I can tell you what the case is, but I really can't discuss it."

Barnes looked at Preston. Preston raised his eyebrows in inquiry, and looked toward the door. Barnes nodded. He turned back to me.

"Any objection to taking a little ride?" he asked.

I considered the proposition. I wondered what would happen if I said no. Somehow, I didn't really feel like finding out. Being a basic coward, in sticky situations my instinct is not to make trouble but just to ride along. In this case, literally.

"O.K.," I said. "Let's go."

We went out to the parking lot. No one paid any attention to us going through the lobby, which made me wonder for the first time how the cops had gotten into my room. I'd have thought if they'd had to inquire for the key at the desk, it would have aroused some curiosity. The fact that no one gave a damn about us seemed to imply that they hadn't.

The cops' car was black and unmarked. Sergeant Preston opened the back door for me. Before he let me in he asked, "You licensed to carry?"

"No."

"You mind if I check?"

"That's your job," I told him.

Preston patted me down for a weapon. When he didn't find one, he let me in the back seat.

The cops got in the car and took off, Preston driving.

The car came out of the parking lot and turned right. I was glad. Wherever else we were going, it wasn't the Dunleavy house.

I wondered where we *were* going. In the direction we were heading there were a number of possibilities, most of them bad. We could have been going to the Weasel's. We could have been going to the Bear's. We could have been going to chat with Mike Sallingsworth, to see how his story compared with mine. We *could* have been going to the casinos to play the slots, but somehow I doubted it.

We didn't do any of those things. The car left Route 30, made a few turns, and pulled up in front of a house on Mediterranean Avenue.

Barnes turned around in the front seat. "You know who lives here?"

"No, I don't."

Barnes nodded. "O.K. Get out."

We went up on the front porch. It turned out to be one of those two-story frame houses that have been divided up into apartments. In the foyer was a row of bells. Barnes pushed one of them. Seconds later there was a buzz, and he pushed open the inner door.

We went up a flight of stairs. Barnes knocked on a door. It opened, and a female voice said, "Yes."

The voice sounded vaguely familiar, but I couldn't place it, and with Barnes and Preston standing in front of me, I couldn't see its owner.

Barnes turned back, put his hand on my shoulder and pushed me forward.

I saw her, and my heart sank. It was Pudgy, from the Photomat.

She looked at me, nodded and said, "That's him."

"Are you sure?" Barnes asked.

"I want to be sure there's no mistake," Barnes said. "This is the man who showed up at your Photomat this morning? This is the man who gave the name Robert Fuller, and took the photographs for the Minton agency?"

"That's right."

Barnes nodded in satisfaction. "Very good. And could you tell me the amount of the bill for those photographs?"

"I added it up, like you asked me," Pudgy said. "It came to one hundred seven dollars and ninety-five cents."

"Excellent," Barnes said. "Just enough."

He turned to me and pulled a pair of handcuffs from his belt. "Stanley Hastings," he said. "You are under arrest." He clamped the handcuffs on my wrists. "The charge is grand larceny. You have the right to remain silent. If you give up the right to remain silent—"

He went through the rest of it, but I didn't really hear him. I was too busy kicking myself in the head. Like a schmuck, I'd done it again. I'd fucked myself.

Somehow I always seem to. And somehow, I always seem to do it just when I think I'm being so smart.

This morning, getting those photographs had seemed like a master stroke. I'd bailed out MacAullif's daughter, got her out of a godawful mess. And I'd done it so easily, and there seemed like no way I could get caught. How the hell was I to know that two people were going to get murdered in the course of the afternoon, blowing the importance of those photographs all out of proportion? But they had, and here I was, fucked again. I'd taken a chance getting the photographs, and it had backfired in my face.

All things considered, I guess I really deserved it. Somehow it was just my fate to be the scapegoat, the asshole, the fool.

And I guess it was only fitting, somehow, what with me being in Atlantic City and all, and having been on the Boardwalk and having taken a Chance, that I should now go directly to Jail, without passing Go and without collecting two hundred dollars.

18

They drove me right to the police station, which was on Bacaharach Avenue in the same building as City Hall. Barnes and Preston ushered me into the station, through the reception area, down a hall, and led me to a uniformed officer at a desk.

"Book him," Barnes said. "Grand larceny."

The cop nodded, fed a form into a typewriter and proceeded to take down the necessary information. I gave him everything he asked for. I wasn't looking for trouble. I had enough already.

When he was finished, he unlocked the handcuffs, led me over to a table and took my fingerprints. I'd been fingerprinted before, so I knew the routine. The guy rolled out some ink on a sheet of Plexiglas, then took my fingers one at a time, inked them, and rolled them onto the appropriate places on the card.

When he was done he gave me a paper towel to wipe my hands and led me into another room to be photographed. He hung a number around my neck and shot me full face. Then he turned me around and shot my profile. I was too distracted to notice whether he got my good side.

I'd never been through the routine before, but I

figured the next procedure would be to take my valuables. Apparently it was, because the cop led me over to a desk with pigeonholes behind it that looked like a lost-and-found.

Barnes appeared as if on cue and said, "Never mind his valuables. This one's going to court."

The cop gave Barnes a look. He said nothing—after all, he was just a desk cop, and Barnes was from Major Crimes—but he did raise his eyebrows, and I didn't blame him.

It was two o'clock in the morning.

The cop shrugged and gave the handcuffs to Barnes, who clapped them on my wrists again. Sergeant Preston appeared out of nowhere and put his hand on my shoulder.

I felt as if I were in a dream somehow, as if none of this was real. As if any moment I'd wake up and find out I was still back in college and hadn't studied for this morning's English final.

Instead, Barnes and Preston steered me outside to the police car again. They put me in the back seat, got in and drove off.

We went a few blocks and pulled into the parking lot of another municipal building. Two cars were parked in the lot, and two men were standing beside 'em, talking. It was dark, but I could see that one of them was a gray-haired, venerable gentleman of about sixty-five, and the other was a dark-haired man approximately my age.

We got out of the car. Barnes and Preston nodded at the two men, who nodded back and went in a side door of the building. We followed.

Someone turned on some lights. We went down some halls and through a few doors, and the next thing I knew the five of us were standing in an otherwise empty courtroom.

The gray-haired gentleman went through a door in the back and reappeared moments later wearing a judge's robes. He took his place at the judge's bench.

Barnes and Preston escorted me up to the bench, and stood with me, one on either side.

The judge leaned down to the dark-haired gentleman and inquired, "Well, Matt, what do we have here?"

Matt, who seemed to be an assistant prosecutor of some sort, had a clipboard in his hand. He referred to it.

"Your Honor, this is the case of one Stanley Hastings, arrested for grand larceny. The charges stem from the unlawful removal of several packages of exposed negatives and developed film belonging to the Minton Detective Agency from the Photomat where they had been left to be processed."

"And how was the theft allegedly accomplished?"

"The defendant secured possession of the film by passing himself off as an employee of the agency, which he is in fact not."

"What evidence do you have to support this?"

"We have the eyewitness testimony of one Sheila Burkes, an employee of the Photomat, who absolutely identifies the defendant as the gentleman who secured the film. We also expect to be able to show that the signature, 'Robert Fuller,' in the Photomat's receipt book for the Minton account, is in the handwriting of the defendant. The defendant is neither Robert Fuller nor an employee of the Minton Agency."

The judge appeared interested. "Is Robert Fuller an employee of the Minton Agency?"

"No, Your Honor, the defendant gave an entirely fictitious name. However, we are not going into the comparative negligence of the employees of the Photo-

mat at this time. I am merely asking that the defendant be bound over for trial."

Something was wrong. I mean aside from the obvious fact that I was about to be indicted for grand
larceny, something was terribly wrong.

The cast of the drama was not complete. There had
been one serious omission. And had I been any less
overwhelmed by the whole situation, had I been even
slightly in possession of my wits and had I not been
basically such a shy, retiring, and unassertive person
to begin with, what I should have been doing was
standing up and screaming, "What the hell is going on
here? Hey! Who's on *my* side? Where the hell's the
public defender? Where's my *attorney*, for Christ's
sake?"

But being who I am and what I am, and given the
circumstances, I just stood there like a clod.

The judge cocked his head and said, "And what
would you recommend with regard to bail?"

Matt, the presumed assistant prosecutor, said, "The
defendant is from out of state."

That did it. My heart sank. Suddenly I realized what
was going on. I was in a Star-Chamber session, and
they were going to fry me. *The defendant is from out
of state.* It was simple, straightforward. I was from out
of state and therefore too big a risk for nominal bail.
Bail would either be denied or set at such an astro-
nomical sum that I could never raise it, even with a
bond.

It was the last straw. Even cowardly, ineffectual
little me was about to protest, when Matt went on,
"However, the defendant is a family man. He has a
wife and child. He resides in New York City and is
employed by a Manhattan law firm. It should be no
problem keeping in touch with him, and under the
circumstances, even should he leave the state, extradi-

tion should not be difficult. Therefore, I recommend that the defendant be released on his own recognizance."

I confess to not having the best poker face in the world. My jaw dropped open.

However, the judge nodded, as if all that made perfect sense, instead of being totally off the wall.

"Very well," he said. "The defendant is hereby bound over for trial, ordered not to leave the jurisdiction of the court, and released on his own recognizance."

He banged the gavel and that was that. Barnes and Preston guided me from the courtroom, the lights were switched off and before it all really had time to register I was back in the car again, totally baffled, and wondering what the fuck was going on.

19

Confused as I was, foggy as I was, tired as I was, when we pulled out of the parking lot and started tooling down Atlantic Avenue, I was still alert enough to realize one thing: we weren't heading home.

And I was still wearing handcuffs.

Now I am admittedly no expert in these matters, but it certainly seemed to me that when cops released you, they took the handcuffs off.

Barnes and Preston hadn't said a word. I realized that was probably a tactic on their part. I realized they were probably waiting for me to ask questions. And I didn't want to give them the satisfaction. But I couldn't help myself. I broke.

"Where we going?" I said.

Barnes turned around in the front seat.

Before he could say anything, Preston turned his head. "Why tell him?" he said.

"Why not?"

"He isn't telling us anything."

"He might."

"Screw him. He had his chance."

"Yeah, but—"

"Aw, screw him."

I knew what was going on. They were playing good

cop/bad cop. Preston was well cast in the role of bad cop, what with being six-foot-four, and all. As he turned to talk to Barnes, I noticed he had a scar on his right cheek. I hadn't seen it before, and I wondered if I only noticed it now because he was playing bad cop.

I was almost glad they were doing it. It was at least a familiar routine, something I recognized from detective fiction. I could deal with it.

They stopped, however. Barnes shrugged, said, "O.K.," and turned around in the seat again.

It was disappointing. It also impelled me to want to talk. I sat on the urge. I contented myself with looking out the window and trying to figure out where we were heading.

We turned right onto Route 40 and headed north. After what seemed an interminable period, we hung a left onto a two-lane blacktop road. A few miles down the road, the car slowed in front of a huge building that looked like a hospital. A sign on the lawn said, "ATLANTIC COUNTY FACILITIES AT NORTHFIELD."

We pulled into the driveway and drove around the building. There was another building in the back. Preston pulled up next to it and parked.

They got me out of the car and led me to the building. A sign on it said, "ATLANTIC CITY PROSECUTOR." We went up a flight of stone steps to a door. The sign on the door said "MAJOR CRIMES."

I couldn't see the theft of some photographs as a major crime, somehow. Murder seemed a little more like it.

We went in the door, down a flight of steps, and through another door, to a small room with two desks. A bleary-eyed cop was sitting at one of them, drinking coffee and looking bored.

"Hi, Hank," Barnes said. "Interrogation free?"

The cop chuckled and shot a look at the clock on the wall. It was after three. "I would think so," he said.

Barnes grinned, and Preston escorted me through a door and into a small room. He took out the key to the handcuffs, which, I must say, was a tremendous relief. He unlocked one wrist. Before I knew what was happening, he threaded the handcuffs through a steel ring attached to the wall, and snapped the cuff back on my wrist again.

On his way out, he cocked his head over his shoulder and said, "Don't go away."

I assumed it was a joke.

I didn't find it funny.

About a half hour later Barnes came in. I wondered if he was still playing good cop.

He was.

He took out a key and unlocked the handcuffs. He pulled out a chair at the table and invited me to sit down. I did. He sat down opposite me.

"Now, Mr. Hastings," he said. "I'm terribly sorry to inconvenience you, but you must understand we are dealing with two murders here. And I have this slight problem. The photographs. The ones which you allegedly took from the Photomat. The detective from the Minton Agency who left them there happens to be one Joseph T. Steerwell, who was murdered yesterday afternoon. Therefore, you can understand our interest in them."

I said nothing.

"Now," Barnes said, "if I remember correctly, you stated that you could not discuss your employer's business relating to the very important case of one—" He referred to his notebook. "One Floyd Watson, who fell down a flight of stairs. I don't recall your mentioning that case having anything to do with Joseph T.

119

Steerwell. Therefore, there's no reason why you shouldn't tell us what you know."

He looked at me expectantly. I still said nothing.

Barnes smiled. "I hate to seem insistent, but I would like to know your connection with Joseph T. Steerwell."

"I'm afraid I can't help you," I said.

"Jesus Christ," came a voice.

I looked. It was Sergeant Preston, standing in the doorway, still playing bad cop. He looked pretty bad standing in that doorway. After all, his head was almost touching the top of the frame.

"Just listen to this guy," he said. " 'I'm afraid I can't help you.' What the hell does he think this is, a game or something? This is a murder investigation."

"I'm sure he's aware of that, Sergeant," Barnes said.

"Of course he's aware of it. He's damn well aware of it." Preston crossed in to the table. "You know what his connection is with Steerwell? I'll tell you. He probably killed him."

Barnes smiled. "I don't think Mr. Hastings would do anything like that."

"Oh, no? Then why ain't he talkin'? This is a murder case. If he's clean, what's he got to hide?"

"I assume he has nothing to hide."

"Then why ain't he talkin'?"

Barnes turned to me. "My partner is a little impetuous, but he does have a point. If you're not involved in this murder, there's no reason why you shouldn't tell us everything you know."

I'd been listening to their conversation, and I must say I found it almost comforting. For one thing, they were talking to each other and not to me, which was a relief. For another, they were playing good cop/bad cop, which was a routine I understood. And understanding the routine made me feel that I could deal with it.

I was about to make some noncommittal response when I had an inspiration.

"Excuse me," I said. "Perhaps I don't understand something here. You see, I'm not a lawyer, so I don't understand all the nuances of the situation. But, you see, I thought the matter was settled. With regard to Joseph T. Steerwell, I mean. If those really were his pictures. I've been indicted on charges of grand larceny, and released pending trial. Correct me if I'm wrong, but it would seem to me that with a criminal matter pending, I am under no obligation to discuss the matter further, and moreover, your attempts to make me do so are a violation of my constitutional rights."

There was a sickening silence.

Barnes looked at Preston. "Well, what do we do now?"

"I'll tell you what I'd like to do now. Whaddya say we drive him to the border, arrest him attempting to leave the jurisdiction of the court, haul him in for jumping bail, rescind it, and put him on ice?"

Barnes smiled ruefully and shook his head. "He doesn't mean that," he told me. "He just gets carried away at times."

"Yeah," Preston said, disgustedly. He turned and walked out the door.

Leaving me alone with good cop. Part of the technique.

"You'll have to excuse Sergeant Preston," Barnes said. "He's a good cop. Double homicides just make him grouchy."

"I can understand that," I said.

"Then you can understand his point of view. Murder is not a game. Someone killed two people. And they shouldn't get away with it."

"I'm with you there."

"Are you? Good. Then let's discuss it. Now I'm a reasonable man. But this bullshit about violating your rights and all—'cause that's what it is, bullshit—that just doesn't sit well. No one wants to violate your rights. All we're concerned with is the murder. Now as far as these pictures are concerned, they're relatively unimportant. As far as we know, they have no connection with the murder. Therefore, as far as the charge of grand larceny goes, if we could clear this murder up, I'm sure that charge could just quietly disappear."

I said nothing.

"So," Barnes said. "You have everything to gain and nothing to lose in telling us everything you know. Unless, of course, those pictures are connected with the murder. Therefore, if you continue to remain silent, I'm forced to conclude that they are."

I shifted my position in the chair. It was a good argument—if you keep quiet you're confirming our suspicions and proving your guilt. I really felt impelled to say something. To at least make a denial. I felt very proud of myself that I didn't.

Barnes sat there, silently, for what seemed like a good minute. Then he sighed.

"All right," he said. "We'll have to draw our own conclusions."

He got up and walked out the door.

I'd just had time to realize that he'd left me alone and unhandcuffed when Preston came in and chained me to the wall again. He wasn't exactly rough about it. Just abrupt. He managed to convey the impression that it could have been rough, had he wanted it to be.

He performed the operation without a word and went out the door again. It occurred to me that he must have been outside the door all the time, listening while Barnes was talking to me, to have come in on cue. I liked that. I mean, I liked the idea that I

122

realized that. It meant that I was still on to their game. Still hip to what they were trying to do.

I started thinking back over the conversation, trying to judge my performance, see how well I was doing. I kind of liked that whole bit I came up with about not being able to discuss the case now that it was pending trial. That had been a pretty good one.

I thought about it some more and I immediately started having doubts. That happens to me a lot. Every time I think I've done something smart, I immediately think, "Wait a minute. Did you really?" 'Cause I'm basically insecure and I always have doubts.

In this case, the doubts came thick and fast. Yeah, suppose I can't talk to 'em since I'm released pending trial. But the thing is, who put me in that position? Barnes and Preston. And they'd done it by means of a middle-of-the-night star-chamber session that was highly irregular to say the least. And they'd had me released on my own recognizance. They hadn't had to do that. They hadn't had to charge me at all. Having charged me, they were under no compulsion to whisk me right before a judge. And then when the judge bound me over for trial, they hadn't had to release me. They could have asked for a stiff bail and clapped me in jail. But they hadn't done that. So what was this about Preston saying he wanted to violate my bail and send me back to jail? That was bullshit, of course. They could have done that in the first place. They didn't want me in jail. They wanted me with them. Well, they had me with them to begin with. They didn't have to go through all that shit, just to get back where they started. So it was all part of the game. But what *was* the game? What were they getting at? Why had they done this?

I realized for all my understanding of the game, I had no idea why it was being played.

I tried to think logically. After all, I taught math once—I'd dealt with logic problems. What was the logic of this situation?

Well, to understand why a person performs an action, consider the consequences of that action. What did they gain?

In this case, what Barnes and Preston had gained was getting me booked for grand larceny. Big deal. What did it get 'em?

I had no idea.

The door opened and Barnes and Preston came in again. They were both drinking coffee. Barnes looked tired. Preston looked tall.

Without a word, Preston unlocked the handcuffs and sat me down at the table. Barnes and Preston sat down on either side. Barnes sipped his coffee, leaned back in his chair.

"Well," he said. "We got the report back from the lab."

That startled me. I blurted, "Lab?"

"Yeah," Preston said. "We're not the only guys you've been keeping up all night. There's people all over New Jersey sipping coffee and cursing you."

"That's hardly fair, Preston," Barnes said.

"Oh, yeah? You know what my wife's gonna say when I get home?"

"Sure: Shit! It's my husband! Get your pants on and hop out the window!"

"That's what *your* wife says. Remember when we were up all night on the Melbourne case?"

"I don't even remember the Melbourne case."

"How could you forget the Melbourne case? That was the nymphomaniac kept claiming she'd been raped."

"Oh, yeah."

"I remember I got home five in the morning, my

wife hops out of bed, says, 'Where the hell you been?'
I said, 'Shit, honey, I been up all night with a nymphomaniac.' She says, 'Don't lie to me. You've been
playing poker with the boys again.' "

Jesus Christ. They'd stopped playing good cop/bad
cop and were doing vaudeville routines. And I knew
why they were doing it. They'd aroused my curiosity
with that crack about the lab, and now they were
letting me stew.

The thing was, it was working.

"What about the lab?" I asked.

"Hey!" Preston said. "Look at this. The clam wants
to talk."

"Is that right?" Barnes said. "Did you have something to say?"

"I just thought you boys came in here to tell me
something. Or did you just want me to play Mr.
Interlocutor?"

Barnes grinned. "You know, Preston, the guy's got
a sense of humor."

"It's probably his only virtue," Preston said.

I was damned if I was gonna ask 'em again.

"Any chance of me getting a cup of that coffee?" I
said.

Barnes and Preston looked at each other.

"Sure," Preston said. "Let's get him a cup of coffee."

Barnes and Preston got up and walked out.

I sat there like a fool. I probably could have figured
everything out there and then—about the lab, I
mean—if I hadn't been so dazed, so bewildered by
what was going on. Jesus Christ, it was as if I were an
audience of one, watching the Barnes and Preston
Show. At any moment now, they'd come tap-dancing
through the door with straw hats and canes. Or perhaps they'd have gone through another metamorpho-

sis. Barnes would come in dribbling a basketball and pass it to Preston who'd slam-dunk it down my throat.

They didn't. They came back with a paper cup full of coffee. Preston handed it to me and the cops sat down. We all sat there drinking coffee. No one said a word. We just sat and waited for someone to do something.

I did.

I began to fidget.

Barnes noticed. "He's fidgeting," he said.

"I noticed that," Preston said.

"All right, damn it," I said. "What about the lab?"

"Ah, the lab," Barnes said. "You tell him, Preston. You took the call."

Preston pulled a notebook out of his pocket.

"Well, after we booked you, we sent your finger-prints down to the lab, to the guys doing the workup on Frederick Nubar. And you know what they found? Your fingerprints are all over the Nubar house. They're on the front doorknob. They're on the rail of the front porch, where someone puked in the bushes. They're on the coffee table in the living room, right next to where the body was found."

Preston looked up from his notes. "And—and this is the one I like—there's a print of your right thumb and index finger on Nubar's wallet. The wallet that was in the hip pocket of the dead man's trousers."

20

Now you know why I am not the world's greatest detective. I have a tendency to lose my head in pressure situations and not think rationally. I mean, come on, what is the most elemental element of any detective story? Fingerprints. But I hadn't thought of that. Couldn't even figure it out when they mentioned the lab.

All right, so I was rattled. It was my second murder of the day. And being overfull of self affairs, my mind did lose it. Who said that? Theseus? Oberon? Shit. I wonder if English lit teachers get into this much trouble. Perhaps I should consider a change of occupation.

". . . If you cannot afford an attorney, one will be appointed for you." Preston finished up the drone. "God, I hate saying that. But we gotta, you see. It's the law."

"Right," Barnes said. "It's the law. And the law must not be broken. You understand that, don't you, Mr. Hastings? Now, as Mr. Preston so aptly says, you have the right to an attorney. You work for an attorney. Maybe you'd like to get him on the phone. Maybe while you have him on the phone, you might explain to him how you're refusing to answer our questions on the grounds that they might pertain to his business.

Specifically, his business with one Frederick Nubar. It might be interesting to find out what he advises you to do with regard to that. So, would you like to call him?"

I considered how Richard would feel about being called at four in the morning. I realized he'd actually love it. You see, Richard has this dream of defending a client in a hopeless murder case. Preferably a guilty one. Richard might be a terrible pain in the ass when I was just a douche-bag investigator dealing with his business, but cast me in the role of a murder suspect, and he'd be a prince.

Yeah. Richard wouldn't have minded a bit.

But I would.

The thing was, I was still protecting Barbara and Harold. Trying to keep them out of it. And I was still trying to keep MacAullif out of it, whether he'd held out on me or not. So, all things considered, I didn't want to talk to Richard any more than I wanted to talk to Barnes and Preston.

Maybe even less.

"Not at the present time," I told Barnes.

"Fine," Barnes said. "Please make a note of that, Preston. Suspect was offered an opportunity to contact his attorney, and declined. Now," he said to me, "having also been duly warned that you don't have to talk to us, I would like to point out that now might be an excellent time for you to do so. Particularly with regard to explaining the presence of your fingerprints on Nubar's wallet. Do you have anything to say?"

I wondered what would happen if I said no. I also wondered what would happen if I tried to explain. I had no idea. But I had a feeling in either case, whatever happened wouldn't be pleasant.

I'd like to have you think that it was my iron will and steel resolve that kept me from cracking then. But actually, it was simply that faced with the two unpleasant alternatives, saying no seemed by far the easiest.

"I have nothing to say," I told him.

Barnes nodded, as if that were exactly the answer he had been expecting. They got up, chained me to the wall again, and walked out.

After that, Barnes and Preston went through another incarnation. They became Greek Furies, flying in the door every now and then to torment the tragic hero, chained to the post.

"Floyd Watson," Preston said, poking his head in the door.

"What about him?"

"We checked up in the log of Aided Accidents, and it's just as you said. The guy fell down the flight of stairs in the casino."

"There you are," I said.

He shrugged. "Yeah. You told us you came down to Atlantic City because Floyd Watson fell down the stairs, and damned if he didn't fall down the stairs."

"I told you so."

"Yeah. Only thing is, the date of the accident. Floyd Watson fell down the flight of stairs the day *after* you got here. So, we're wondering how you knew this guy was going to fall down the stairs."

Preston grinned at me and ducked out.

Barnes ducked in a short while later.

"Julie Blessing," he said.

"Who?"

"The secretary at Nubar's. She identifies you as the man who called on Nubar at the office yesterday."

I stared at him. "Identifies?" I said. "What do you mean, identifies? No one's been in to see me. How the hell could she identify me?"

"I'm sorry," Barnes said, "but, you see, we have no facilities for line-ups here at Major Crimes, so we do it with pictures. Miss Blessing picked your mug shot from out of a group of six."

"I see," I said.

"Yeah," Barnes said. "She says you came in, gave the improbable name Phil Collins and then decided not to wait."

"Oh."

Barnes smiled, innocently. "She said you must have decided to see him later," he said and ducked out.

Preston was next.

"Felicia Holt."

"Who?"

"Receptionist at Minton's Detective Agency. She I.D.'s you as the man who came in twice looking for Joseph T. Steerwell, the last time on the day of the murder."

"Oh."

"She says you came to the agency for the first time, three days ago, spoke to Minton and hired Steerwell to do a job for you."

"She what!?" I blurted.

"She I.D.'s you as the guy who hired Steerwell. She assumes it had something to do with the pictures."

"Son of a bitch!" I said.

"Anything the matter?" Barnes said, coming in the door.

"I don't know," Preston said. "I was just telling him how the Holt woman identified him as the guy who hired Steerwell, and he went bananas."

"They do that sometimes when they get I.D.'d. It's 'cause they realize they're caught."

"Bullshit," I said. "That goddamn woman is full of prunes. I never hired Steerwell. I—"

I realized I was blowing it. I stopped myself.

"Too bad," Preston said. "I thought he was going to tell us something."

"Guess not," Barnes said.

They turned and headed for the door.

"Wait a minute," I said.

They stopped.

"Yes," Barnes said.

"This guy who hired Steerwell. Did he talk to anyone else at the agency?"

"Oh, sure," Barnes said. "According to the secretary, you spoke to Minton himself. Then Minton passed you along to Steerwell."

"Well, there you are," I said. "Why don't you ask Minton if I hired him?"

"He's in Las Vegas," Preston said. "When he gets back, we certainly will."

"When's he coming back?"

"Tomorrow."

I groaned. "Great."

The Furies smiled at me and went out the door.

I sat there, cursing my fate. Ordinarily being mistaken for a thirty year old would have been flattering, but not now. All right, both Harold Dunleavy and I had dark hair and blue eyes and were about the same height and weight. And maybe he looked a little older than he was, and maybe I always do feel I look a little younger.

But Jesus Christ.

That damn fool woman.

I was still thinking this when my Furies returned. They came in together this time, so it must have been something good. I braced myself.

"Priscilla Martin," Barnes said.

"Who?"

"Steerwell's next-door neighbor."

"Oh."

That would be Miss Busybody. I'd been wondering when they'd get around to her.

"Miss Martin," Barnes said, "identifies you as the gentleman she saw at Steerwell's house on the day of the murder."

No surprise there. I'd been sure that she would.

"Yeah," Preston said. "She says you were the man she saw running in and out of the house just before she saw the woman come out with the gun."

21

Richard hit town like a tornado. Also like a high roller. The first inkling I got of his arrival was hearing a buzz of voices from the outer room, in which the only identifiable word was stretch-limo. I later found out Richard had also taken a helicopter and a Lear jet. With all of that, he probably shaved a good fifteen minutes off the time it would have taken him just to drive down.

I'd called Richard right after Barnes dropped the bomb about Miss Busybody. Call me a coward if you will, but somehow that was just more than I could take. The thing was, the thought flashed through my mind: "New Jersey doesn't have the death penalty, does it?" And I figured if I was thinking along those lines, maybe it was time to call a lawyer.

I had trouble getting through. Wendy/Cheryl wasn't too keen on connecting me, what with me missing calling in and all. But after she'd bawled me out a good bit, Richard got on the phone to bawl me out too.

"I got arrested," I said.

That calmed him right down. "What's the charge?"

"I've been indicted for grand larceny."

"Oh," Richard said, and I could hear the interest

oozing out of him. "I'm really rather busy at the moment, and—"

"And now I'm being held on suspicion of murder."

"I'll be right there."

He was, too. It seemed an eternity to me, but that wasn't because of any failing on Richard's part. Everything that could have been done, he'd done. For a man who begrudged me every roll of film on my expense account, he'd certainly gone all out.

Right after the stretch-limo murmur, I heard a door slam and then a familiar, high-pitched nasal bark, after a few minutes of which, Richard strode into the room, followed by a rather dazed-looking Barnes and Preston.

Richard took one look at me and stopped dead. He wheeled on the officers.

"Chained?" Richard said, with an inflection I couldn't even begin to imitate. *"Chained* to the *wall?"*

"Well, you see," Barnes said. "We have no holding cells here, so—"

Richard wasn't about to listen.

"I need to confer with my client," he snapped. "I need to confer with him alone. You will provide a room. I hereby serve notice that if that room is bugged, or if one word of that conversation is overheard in any way, it will constitute a violation of my client's rights, and he will walk on any charge whatsoever, up to and including murder."

The thing about Richard is, I don't think he really knows that much law, I think a lot of what he says is bullshit, but when he says it, people listen. Two minutes later we were sitting in a small room with a closed door.

"All right," Richard said. "What's the story?"

"You gotta understand," I told him. "I'm protecting someone."

"Who?"

"Clients."

"You work for me."

"Yeah, but I'm on vacation and I got some clients, and that's who I'm protecting."

"Who are they?"

"I can't tell you that."

"I'm your lawyer."

"I know that."

"And you're in deep shit."

"I know that, too."

"So this is not the time to play button-button-who's-got-the-button. What's the story?"

I told him. I told him the whole thing. I just didn't give him Harold and Barbara's names. I didn't mention MacAullif at all.

Richard listened without interruption until I was finished. Then he blinked and said, "That's incredible."

"Isn't it?"

"No, I mean it. It's really incredible. You have two clients, the man and the wife, who are not acting together. In fact, part of your job is trying to protect the wife from the husband. They are both murder suspects, and one of the two of 'em probably did it. And these are the people you're protecting."

"That's right."

Richard leaned back in his chair and shook his head. "This," he said, "is why I confine my practice to litigation."

"If you'd prefer me to call another lawyer—"

"No, no, no," Richard said. "I can handle it. I can't *follow* it, but I can handle it. You see, any situation can be resolved by proper analysis. For instance, my analysis of this situation leads to one inescapable conclusion: the man and the wife may be your clients, but it is obvious neither one of them hired you."

"This is true."

"So who did?"

"No one."

"What?"

"No one hired me."

"I don't understand."

"I'm doing this as a favor for a friend."

Richard cocked his head at me. "Do you mean to tell me that this whole deplorable situation is the result of you doing a favor for a friend?"

"I suppose so."

Richard shook his head. "I was right. You're a total moron."

"Thank you."

Richard sighed. "All right. Setting aside for the moment the fact that the entire situation is utterly absurd, let's examine it rationally for a moment."

"You're welcome to try."

"Thank you. Aside from the grand larceny charge, of which you have the advantage of actually being guilty, your problem is simply a case of mistaken identity. Which, incidentally, would help me immensely if I really wanted to find out who your clients were. I'd just look around town for a married couple where the husband was a fortyish douche-bag with dark hair and a goony-looking expression."

"Thanks a lot."

"Don't mention it. At any rate your problem is simple. Or as simple as it can be, seeing as how you didn't kill either of these people. The only thing that ties you to Nubar is the fingerprints on the wallet. And the fact you made inquiries about him. The fingerprints mean nothing. They're not dated. They could have been made at any time. I'd have fun arguing the point. They're damaging, I'll admit, but they're not enough to hold you on. And the nice thing is, they have a much better case against you for killing Steerwell."

"That's a nice thing?"

"Absolutely. Because that makes it the main case. The one they concentrate on. The one they try to build on. So if we can knock it down, their whole theory about the two murders collapses."

"I see," I said. I didn't really, but Richard had paused there, and was looking at me, and I realized that was what I was supposed to say.

"Now, let's look at the case they have against you for killing Steerwell. The damaging witness is the one you call Miss Busybody. That's the one who says she saw you run in and out of Steerwell's house at about the time of the murder."

"That's right."

"The guy who actually did go in and out—she get a good look at this guy?"

"Obviously not. She'd seen me up close earlier in the day. Then she saw this guy run in and out. She didn't get a good look, but she assumed it was me."

Richard nodded. "She shouldn't be too hard to break on cross-examination if it came to that. What kind of car does this guy drive?"

"Why? You trying to find my client through his automobile?"

"No. I'm trying to break down the identification. What kind of car do *you* drive?"

"A Toyota."

"This other guy drive a Toyota or anything like it?"

"Not even close."

"See, that should do it right there. If this witness had really been paying attention to this guy, she'd have seen what car he got in. Then I could show it wasn't yours. How could she have made that mistake, by the way? If, as she says, she was so interested in this guy, she'd have watched him till he drove off."

I thought a minute. "When I was there, Steerwell wasn't home. There was no car in the driveway, so she could have seen my car just fine. When the other guy was there, Steerwell's car was in the driveway. So if the guy parked in the street, slightly beyond it, Steerwell's car would have blocked it from view."

Richard nodded. "Still, she should have seen it, and I'll bet I can crucify her with it. That's all well and good. But it's only useful if the thing comes to trial. And that's what we are attempting to avoid."

I felt that was a less than completely sincere statement. Richard would have loved to go to trial.

"So," Richard said. "The other witness, from the Minton Agency. How well did she see you?"

"Barely at all. Both times I was in there she was typing. The first time she glanced up once briefly just to tell me to get lost. The second time she never looked up at all."

"But she swears you were the guy who was in there the day before, talked to Minton and hired Steerwell?"

"Right."

"Then the situation is simple," Richard said.

He smiled, got up and walked out of the room.

I sat and waited.

About an hour later the door opened again. I looked up expectantly, but it wasn't Richard. It was Barnes and Preston.

"Where's my lawyer?" I said.

Preston shrugged. "He went back to New York."

My heart sank. "What?"

"He had business to attend to, and he'd already wasted half a day. He's on his way home. He asked us to make his apologies."

I couldn't believe it. Richard quitting just like that.

It was just another in the string of emotional shocks
I'd been getting lately.

I got another.

Barnes said, "You can go."

I blinked. "What?"

"You're free to go."

One thing about me is, besides being a coward, I am
not really emotionally stable. I hold together as long
as I can, and then I crack up. And in this case, I was
way overdue.

I started giggling. I couldn't stop. I just sat there,
giggling uncontrollably.

Barnes and Preston just stood there staring at me.
Neither said a word. They both looked as if they were
observing some totally weird phenomenon, which, I
guess, they were.

Finally I got control. "I'm sorry," I said.

"Are you all right?" Barnes asked.

"No, but I'm as all right as I'm going to be. I'm
sorry. I just don't quite understand."

"Well," Barnes said. "Your attorney—this Rosenberg—is quite a character, if you don't mind my saying
so. And he makes a very interesting case. He implies,
without actually saying so, that your silence in this
matter is not because of any guilt on your part, but
because you are protecting some unnamed client. It's
good he implies that rather than states it, because
frankly, we wouldn't like that at all. But setting that
aside, here's the situation.

"Your attorney claims that it is possible that you
had some dealings with Frederick Nubar—which he is
not willing to admit—which would account for your
fingerprints on his wallet. However he categorically
denies that you killed him. He claims that this whole
situation is a result of mistaken identity. That apparently you and the man who hired Steerwell and who

ran in and out of his house are somewhat similar in appearance. He dismisses the fact that both witnesses picked your photo out of the line-ups. He claims that had the photo of the other man been in there, both witnesses would have unerringly picked him."

Barnes grinned. "And here's where it gets interesting. I must say this guy has a flair. He says since we're in Atlantic City and gambling's legal and all, he'll bet his whole case on the fact that when this Minton, who was the only one who had a good look at the guy, gets back from Vegas, he'll say it wasn't you."

"And," Preston said, "then he says, 'Charge him or release him.' And he points out if we charge you, and then this guy Minton comes back from Vegas and blows the identification, we are going to look like the two stupidest cops in New Jersey."

"Not that that bothers us any," Barnes put in quickly. "We are concerned with upholding the law, not how we look in the press."

"Naturally," Preston said.

"So," Barnes said. "Your attorney says if we hold off charging you till this Minton gets back, you will be not only willing but eager to participate in clearing up the matter of the identification."

"I see," I said. It was all I seemed to ever get to say in this damn case, in which I didn't see a thing.

"So," Barnes said. "You're free to go."

I took a breath. "You're telling me I can walk out of here?"

"Sure. We've even arranged a ride for you back to your hotel."

"I see," I said again.

But I didn't get up.

"Is anything wrong?" Barnes asked.

"I'm sorry," I said. "But everything's happening very fast. This is all a little much. I hate to seem so stupid, but I want to be sure I understand this. You're telling me that there are no charges against me other than the grand larceny one that's already been brought, and that I'm free to walk out of here right now?"

"That's right," Barnes said.

"Fine," I said. "Then let's talk."

22

After all they'd put me through, I must say I was pretty pleased with myself at that moment. Because Barnes and Preston were stunned. They stood there, gaping, looking just as stupid as I'd been looking before.

It was wonderful.

Preston recovered first. "Son of a bitch," he murmured. "The revenge of the clam!"

"Well, what do you know," Barnes said.

"Why don't you boys sit down," I suggested.

Barnes and Preston looked at each other.

"I don't know what's going on," Barnes said. "But I'm willing to ride along. Shall we?"

Barnes and Preston pulled out chairs and sat down.

"That's fine," I said. "Now, gentlemen, I'm very tired, as are we all, and I would very much like to go home, but before I go I would like to clear up one or two points."

"Certainly," Barnes said. He and Preston were still regarding me as if I were from another planet, but they were being very polite.

"All right," I said. "Now look. I'm mighty happy with being released and all that, and you're mighty nice guys and all that, and Richard's one hell of a lawyer and all that, but just between you and me, I think it's bullshit. What you just told me, I mean. About why you're letting me go.

"Now, I'll tell you what I think. I think the reason you're letting me go is, you know you're not going to get anything out of me, so you're hoping I'll lead you to those pictures. Or to whoever it is I'm protecting. And what I wanted to say is, don't. Don't put me under surveillance. I don't like people looking over my shoulder, I'm not going to lead you to anything. It's gonna be a big waste of time and manpower and a major pain in the ass."

Preston looked at Barnes. "Jesus, look at the balls on this guy."

"No," Barnes said. "Let him talk. Go ahead. I presume what you want to do now is explain why putting you under surveillance would do no good."

"Exactly," I said. "Now, as you know, officially I have nothing to say about this investigation. Having said that, if you guys would like to talk hypothetically and off the record, I see no reason why we couldn't discuss the case."

"Hypothetically and off the record is how we usually talk," Barnes said.

"Then, hypothetically and off the record, let me say this. If I were protecting a client, I would feel obligated to that client, and I sure wouldn't do anything that would tell you about him or lead you to him. So if I'm placed under surveillance, it will do no good.

"On the other hand, I don't believe in murder. And if it should turn out that someone I was protecting was guilty of murder, I'd stop protecting them.

"However, there would be no way for me to find out if this person was guilty if you had me under surveillance and I couldn't contact him."

"I see," Barnes said. I was delighted to have someone say that besides me.

"Good," I said. "Now then, with regard to your murders, while I don't know what was actually going on, I'd be delighted to make some suppositions."

"Feel free," Barnes said.

"There were two guns."

"I beg your pardon?"

"There were two murder weapons. Each guy was killed with a different gun. Or to put it another way, the gun found at Steerwell's didn't kill Nubar."

Barnes looked at me. "How do you know that?"

"Because Steerwell died first."

Barnes and Preston looked at each other.

"I don't recall releasing any autopsy reports," Barnes said.

"Neither do I," said Preston. "How do you know that?"

I shrugged. "We're talking hypothetically here, remember?"

"Anything else?" Barnes said.

"Yeah. The gun found at Steerwell's had a silencer."

"How do you figure that?"

"Because the moron who I.D.'d me going into Steerwell's didn't hear a shot."

"Interesting," Barnes said. "Anything else?"

"Yeah. When you traced the serial number on the gun it did you no good. You found out it had been reported stolen, either by a private owner or by a sporting goods store, at least two or three years ago."

"I know why he's doing this," Preston said. "He's not telling us anything. He's feeding us theories about stuff he wants to know, hoping we'll confirm or deny them."

Preston was dead right. I was making logical deductions that anyone could have made from the known facts, and hoping to get a nibble.

"Well, it was worth a try," I said.

"Do you have anything else hypothetical, in the spirit of cooperation?" Barnes asked, somewhat ironically.

"Not at the present time," I said. "In fact, if it's all the same with you, I'll take you up on that ride now."

"Certainly," Barnes said.

We got up.

"And just in case you should choose to disregard my advice about putting me under surveillance," I said, "for the information of the cops assigned to the task, I am going home and going to bed."

A cop drove me back to the hotel. He didn't try to talk to me on the way, and I didn't try to talk to him. I was too damn tired.

I went up to my room and flopped down on the bed. I was really beat.

Before I passed out, I made a call. I figured that even though MacAullif had blown my cover with his daughter, after all he was only human, and he was vitally concerned, and he had a right to know.

If he didn't know already. I wondered about that, too.

"Yeah," MacAullif growled.

"I have news, and it ain't good," I said. "Unless your daughter's already told you."

"What's that supposed to mean?"

"Well, she's your daughter and all. I assume she tells you things."

"What the hell are you talking about? What things?"

"I guess you haven't heard. The detective Harold hired to spy on your daughter's been murdered."

"What!?"

"Not to mention the loan shark Harold was in hock to. He's been murdered, too."

MacAullif hadn't heard. His surprise was genuine, I'd swear it.

"Jesus Christ!" he said. "Are you serious?"

"Absolutely."

"Oh, my God! This is awful!" There was a pause, then MacAullif said, "Listen. What ever you do—keep Harold out of it."

I'm afraid I chuckled. I was thinking of Miss Busybody's identification.

"I'm doing one hell of a job of that."

23

I told MacAullif everything. Everything except the interlude between the tree surgeon and his daughter. Of course, that left a few glaring gaps in the story. Like the bit about me getting indicted for grand larceny. But I told him the rest of it. And even without the bit about the pictures, there was still a lot to tell.

"Jesus Christ!" MacAullif said.

"My sentiments exactly," I told him.

"Why didn't you call me before?"

"You're a police officer, and I have to tell you that? You only get one phone call. Under the circumstances, I opted to call my lawyer."

"He really came down there? That Rosenberg guy? He came down there and kicked ass?"

"After a fashion."

"I'd have liked to have seen it. I remember some of the things he said to me."

"I'm glad you're so amused. It happens your daughter and your son-in-law are in deep shit, and I'm in serious danger of taking a fall for double homicide."

"I know, I know."

"Now, I know I said I'd do you a favor, and I'd certainly like to help your son-in-law out, but that doesn't include taking a murder rap for him."

"I just don't understand how that happened," MacAullif said.

"It's perfectly easy to understand," I said. That was pretty ballsy of me, seeing as how I didn't really understand anything. "Unless Harold is actually guilty, which I can't really discount, he was set up to be a fall guy."

"By whom?"

"I don't know. But the point is, if he was, then the witnesses have fucked up and identified me. Which elevates me into the same position."

"True."

"The saving grave is Minton. When he gets back, I should be off the hook. Of course, Harold may be on it."

"Shit."

"So there we are. Two people have been murdered. Your daughter had a motive for murdering one. Your son-in-law had a motive for murdering the other. However, the cops seem to have elected me for both. Now, I know I said I'd do you a favor and all that, but this is going a little far."

"What a mess."

"Exactly. And how did we get into it?"

"What do you mean?"

"Your daughter went out to see Steerwell yesterday. I don't know what she did when she got there, but she might have killed him."

"Barbara wouldn't do that."

"Maybe not. But her fingerprints are on the murder weapon. She was also seen with it in her hand. So my question is, why did she do it?"

"Why did she do what?"

"Why did she go out there?"

"I don't know what you mean?"

"Yes, you do. Aside from Harold, you and I are the

only ones who knew that he hired Steerwell. And I sure didn't tell her."

There was a silence on the line.

"Which means you did," I said.

"Well, I—"

"Of course you did. I don't blame you for that. She's your daughter, it's family, it's personal. But you didn't tell me you told her. You held out on me. You made me play it wide open, like an asshole, without knowing what I was doing. And that's how we got into this mess. If I'd known you'd told her, I could have headed the situation off."

"What situation?"

"Her going out there."

"Oh, yeah," MacAullif said. "Then *why* did she go out there?"

"I just told you. Because you spilled the beans. Because you told her Steerwell was on to her."

"Yeah, but why would that make her panic? Why would she rush out there? What did she have to hide?"

"What do you mean?"

"I'm talking about holding out on people," MacAullif said. "I have asked you repeatedly what happened while Steerwell was watching my daughter's house. And you told me nothing. I didn't believe you then, and I don't believe you now. And I didn't believe my daughter on the phone when she told me nothing happened, either.

"Something happened while Steerwell was watching the house, and that's why he knocked off at noon. He wasn't hired for any half day. He got what he came for. And that's why my daughter was in such a panic when I told her she was being watched, and that's why she rushed out there. And that's why you're holding out on me."

"Listen—" I said.

"Listen, bullshit! I'm a cop, and I'll always be a cop, and I know when people are holding out on me, and I've known about you for some time. Now cut the shit and tell me what happened."

I sighed.

"All right," I said. "It appears your daughter has formed a liaison with a young man."

"Then why the fuck couldn't you have told me that?" MacAullif cried in exasperation. "Jesus Christ, my daughter's twenty-eight years old. Her husband's running around with every skirt in town. You think this is the crime of the century? You think this is the most earth-shattering news to come down the pike in twenty years? You think my heart couldn't stand it?"

I could picture him shaking his head, pityingly.

"Jesus Christ," he said. "You must be the most puritanical son of a bitch I've ever run into. What do you think this is, the fucking Middle Ages? You think you're some white knight on a charger, dashing off to save the young lady's honor? What are you, a moron? I mean, Jesus Christ, I cannot believe you let this situation develop over a stupid thing like that."

I said nothing. I felt once again like a total asshole, which I guess is the role I'm destined to play in life.

"All right," MacAullif said. "So I held out on you, and you held out on me, and now everything's all fucked up. Well, that's behind us now. Let's figure out what the fuck we're gonna do. So tell me what happened."

"What do you mean?"

"What do you think I mean? That morning. The detective and my daughter."

"Well, he was there when a young man came to the house."

"I know that. Did he take any pictures?"

Shit. He would ask me that.

"Yes he did."

"Shit. Does Harold know?"

"No."

"Where are the pictures?"

"I have them."

"What!?"

"I have the pictures. I stole them from the Photomat where Steerwell left them to be developed."

"No shit! I take it all back what I said about you being a moron. Damn good work."

"Yeah, except the cops know it. That's another way they got onto me. I've been indicted for grand larceny."

"For a roll of pictures?"

"Thirteen rolls. I had to pick up the whole work order for the Minton Agency."

"So you've seen the pictures?"

"Yeah."

"What do they show?"

"That your daughter seemed to like the gentleman in question."

"Shit. You burned them, of course?"

I groaned. What an asshole. I was getting a lock on the chump of the month award. It hadn't even occurred to me.

"I said, you burned them, didn't you?"

"No."

"No? You mean the cops have them?"

"No. I mailed them to myself General Delivery."

"Up here?"

"No. Here in Atlantic City."

MacAullif thought that over.

"O.K. That's good. But we gotta get them out of there and burn them up without the cops finding out about them. And they're sure to be following you. That's a problem."

"There's another problem," I told him.

"What's that?"

"One of the other rolls of film happens to be shots of one Frederick Nubar, deceased."

"Holy shit," MacAullif said. "You mean Steerwell was tailing Nubar? That is something the police should know."

"Yeah. Except for one thing," I said.

"What's that?"

"If they did, the way things stand now, they'd figure *I* had hired Steerwell to tail him."

MacAullif thought that over.

"What a fucking mess," he said.

"Well," I said, "at least we still agree on something."

24

I left a wake-up call for eight o'clock that night. I got up, showered, put on a suit and tie, went down to the lobby and looked up an address in the phone book, drove downtown, bought a pint of bourbon, and made a social call.

It was a second floor walk-up on Ventnor Avenue. Mike Sallingsworth opened the door. He flinched slightly when he recognized me, but that was his only reaction.

He cocked his head at me. "You here to punch me in the nose?" he asked.

I pulled the pint of bourbon out of the bag. "No. I'm here to buy you a drink."

"I prefer that," he said.

He swung the door open and gestured to me to come in.

We sat down in a small, modestly furnished living room. The furniture was old and tattered. It occurred to me Sallingsworth hadn't been pulling down two hundred dollars a day very often.

"I'll get some glasses," he said.

"Get one," I told him. "I don't drink this stuff."

He looked at me. "You *sure* you're a detective?" he said.

"Not at all," I told him.

He went into the kitchen and came back with an empty glass. No ice. No water. He poured a slug of bourbon in and gulped it down. I had a feeling the glass was because he considered it a social occasion. If I hadn't been there he'd have gulped it straight from the bottle.

Sallingsworth poured another shot, held it up, looked at it, then looked at me.

"I don't mean to look a gift horse in the mouth," he said. "But I'm wondering about the purpose of this little visit."

"I've been talking to some of the boys from Major Crimes," I said. "Barnes and Preston."

Sallingsworth nodded. "Good men."

"Yeah, I thought so. Very entertaining."

Sallingsworth slugged down a second shot of whisky and poured another.

"You understand why I had to talk to 'em," he said. "This being a double homicide, and all."

"Oh absolutely," I said. "No problem there. But seeing as how this is a double homicide and all, and seeing as how you seem to be the prime source of information in this town, I thought you and I should have a little talk."

He downed a third shot of bourbon, exhaled happily, and looked at me.

"Barnes and Preston know you're here?"

"I consider it highly likely. They released me, but they're probably having me followed."

"Don't you know?"

"No."

"You're a detective."

"Yeah, but I'm a lousy one."

He nodded judiciously. "That does make it harder. But if they're having you followed, they'll know you came here."

"This is true."

"And they'll ask me what you wanted."

"And you'll tell 'em I came here to bawl you out for talking to them in the first place."

He thought that over. "Is that what you plan to do?"

"No."

"Then what do you want?"

"Information."

"My rates are two hundred dollars a day, plus expenses."

"Your rate's a pint of bourbon and my good will."

He grinned. "Right you are. What you need to know?"

"You familiar with Tallman's Casino?"

"Sure. Newest one on the strip. Opened less than a year ago. Seems to be making a go of it."

"How about a distinguished gentleman, fifty to sixty years old, white hair, razor cut sideburns, gold medallion, and walks around the place with an entourage."

Sallingsworth took another shot.

"That would be Tallman himself."

"I thought it might be. What do you know about him?"

"No one knows that much about him. Of course, there are rumors."

"Such as?"

Sallingsworth seemed to have forgotten the glass. He took a slug straight from the bottle.

"One rumor is that he's mob connected."

"Oh, yeah?"

"Yeah. Another rumor is that he isn't."

"What's that supposed to mean?"

He looked at me sharply. "You know anything about casinos?"

"Only that I shouldn't leave my money in 'em."

He nodded. "That's a hard thing to learn. Well, a casino hotel is an expensive proposition to get going. I mean, getting the land, getting the zoning permit, building the damn thing, outfitting it, hiring the personnel. It's a major undertaking."

"So?"

"So, if Tallman's mob connected, there's no problem, because the money's there. If Tallman's *not* mob connected, the question is, where's the money come from? Nobody puts up umpty million dollars out of their own pocket to build a casino. We're talking mortgages, bank loans, bonds, all that sort of shit. And when you're talking stuff like that, the sixty-four dollar question always is, is the guy good for it?

"Now, in Tallman's case, as I understand it, his collateral is mostly in the form of cash. Now if that cash is coming from the mob, well that's fine, 'cause there's an unlimited source of it. But if it isn't, that's something else.

"So you see, the rumor that Tallman's *not* mob connected is the one that hurts him."

It was all Greek to me. I've never had any money in my life, and my biggest problem is balancing my checkbook. The financial end of it I understood not at all. But I got the gist of what he was saying.

"All right," I said. "Tell me this. Is there any connection between Tallman and Nubar?"

Sallingsworth looked at me in surprise.

"Absolutely not," he said.

"How can you be so sure?"

"Because Tallman wouldn't go near him."

"Why?"

"It would be suicide."

"How come?"

He took another swig from the bottle. "You don't understand this at all, do you?"

"I'm afraid I don't."

"Well, let me try to explain. Nubar is a notorious loan shark. I know it, the cops know it, everybody knows it. It's common knowledge." He grinned. "That's why I was able to give you the information so cheap. But here's the point. For Tallman to have his name connected with Nubar would be a disaster. It would be a scandal of epic proportions. Tallman's whole operation exists on the strength of the fact that he's solvent. For Tallman to be connected with Nubar, a notorious loan shark, in the eyes of everyone would be taken as proof that he is *not* solvent, that he is in serious financial difficulty. And you know what would happen then? His loans would be called in. His financial backing would disappear. And Tallman's Casino would come tumbling down."

Jesus Christ. I tried to think back to all the pictures I'd looked at. The pictures of the King and the Bear. There'd been a lot of pictures of the King, but very few of the Bear. But the thing was, had they ever been together?

I couldn't recall.

I left Sallingsworth with the bottle and drove straight home. But I must admit, if I could have been certain the cops weren't following me, and it hadn't been the middle of the night, and the post office hadn't been closed, I would have loved to have swung by and asked if they had a package for one Stanley Hastings at General Delivery.

25

I woke up the next morning wondering what the fuck to do. The problem, of course, was I was afraid I was being followed. And as I'd told Sallingsworth, I can't spot a shadow to save my life. And if the cops were following me, I couldn't think of anything that was safe for me to do. I certainly wasn't going to drive by the Dunleavy house. And it was a little early to check out the casino—I couldn't imagine Tallman being there in the morning. And I wasn't sure if I wanted to lead the cops to Tallman or not.

When you came right down to it, I finally realized, even if the cops *weren't* following me, I wasn't sure what I wanted to do.

I thought about it, and the way I saw it, all I could really do was hang out and wait for Minton to get back from Las Vegas and get me off the hook. That would probably pull the cops off my tail, and then I'd be free to operate.

I thought about it some more and decided, hell, it's a nice day, I'm going to the beach.

I put on my swimming suit, which Alice had thoughtfully packed for me, along with a pair of tennis shoes and a t-shirt, got in my car, and drove downtown.

FAVOR

I pulled into the garage at Tallman's Casino—God bless free parking—left all my valuables in the glove compartment, locked the car and put on the code alarm.

I walked through the casino, resisting the one-armed bandits, and went out the back door to the Boardwalk. I strolled along the Boardwalk till there was an opening down to the beach. I wondered if this stretch of beach was reserved for Tallman's guests only, if someone would challenge my right to be there, and kick me off.

No one did. I pulled off my shirt and my shoes and socks, stuffed my ignition key into the toe of a shoe, and walked down into the water.

It was great. I waded out into the surf, playing "Wave, wave, don't get my knee," a game I play with my son Tommie, when we vacation at the seashore. By the time I got up to "Wave, wave, don't get my chest," a big one came and hit me in the face, and I was all the way in.

I tried riding the waves for a while, but they weren't really big enough, and I wound up scraping a lot of skin off my stomach. So I waded out just beyond where the waves were breaking and stood there, bobbing up and down as they rolled by me before crashing onto the shore.

I wondered if I was being followed. It was a happy thought. I could imagine the cops, even now, calling back to Major Crimes: "Send me a bathing suit. Yes, damn it, a bathing suit."

I stayed in the water for some time.

And did some thinking.

What I thought about mostly was what would happen when Minton came back. He would exonerate me, which was good, but in doing so, he'd probably pull Harold Dunleavy right into it. I wondered if Harold had been stupid enough to give his right name. I figured he hadn't. If he had and it was in the agency records, the cops would have followed up on it and found him, and, when confronted with Harold Dunleavy, even that stupid secretary would have picked him over me.

The more I thought about it, the more convinced I became that Harold Dunleavy's name was not in the agency records. But that led to another unsettling thought: in all probability, there was *no* name in the agency records. Because if there had been, Barnes and Preston would have sprung it on me. They'd have popped in the door saying, "Julius Gottsagoo," just like they'd confronted me with "Phil Collins" and "Robert Fuller," the other aliases I'd allegedly used.

I couldn't imagine a firm keeping no records at all. After all, they would want to be paid for their work.

So, thinking along those lines, I came up with my worst-case scenario: Minton would return from Vegas. He would take one look at me and say, "No, that's not the guy." Then he would reach in his jacket pocket, pull out his notebook, and say, "I have it right here. The man who hired me is Harold Dunleavy, of Absecon."

I stayed in the water until I started to shrivel up like a prune. Then I went back, got my car, and drove back to the hotel.

There was a cop waiting for me.

"Barnes wants to see you," he said.

I was sure that he did. That probably meant Minton was back in town. That figured.

What didn't figure was why a cop was waiting for me at the hotel. If Barnes was having me followed, he wouldn't need to send a cop there to wait for me.

He'd just have one of the boys on the job pass on the message. So it appeared Barnes was taking me at my word and leaving me alone.

Unless that's what he wanted me to think, and that's why he'd done it.

It's hard when you start double-thinking yourself.

The cop drove me out to Major Crimes. He took me inside to the same room where they'd kept me before. He didn't chain me to the wall, though, which I found encouraging. He went out and left me alone.

A few minutes later Barnes and Preston came in, escorting a bald, fiftyish-looking gentleman in a wilted suit. I figured he was Minton, and I figured right.

The cops didn't talk to me, they talked to him.

"Now, Mr. Minton," Barnes said. "I know you've already seen the picture, but we want to be absolutely sure about this. So, please, take a good look at him."

"I'm sure," Minton said. "There's no question about it."

"We want to be sure there's no mistake."

"There's no mistake."

Barnes and Preston looked at each other. They did not look happy. I knew how they felt. With the secretary and Miss Busybody already having made the identification, this had to be a real kick in the ass.

"You're absolutely sure of the identity of the man who hired you?" Barnes said.

"How many times do I have to tell you?" Minton said. "Yes, I'm absolutely sure."

"And can you tell us what name the man gave you?"

"Of course," Minton said. "I have it right here."

It was just as I'd imagined it in my worst-case scenario. Minton reached into his jacket pocket and pulled out a small, leather-bound notebook.

"I keep all my appointments in here," Minton said. "So there's absolutely no question of mistake."

He riffled through the pages.

"Here we are," he said, pointing to it. "I have it written right here. And it's just as I told you. The man who employed me was one Stanley Hastings, the man standing right there."

26

I believe I've already mentioned that I'm not the world's greatest detective. I would even go so far as to say I'm not in the top ten. If the truth be known, I need all the help I can get. And I must admit, I am not very good at complex and baffling crimes. Simple crimes are a little bit more in my line. And even then I'm not too good at figuring them out. Usually, what it takes for me to crack a case, is for someone to tell me who did it.

I have to admit, Minton's statement came as a bit of a shock. And my initial reaction was the one you would expect: total panic. I once again felt the feeling of cold, clammy fear, the feeling I had felt when I learned Miss Busybody had identified me. I must say it was worse this time, because it was so unexpected. Not that Miss Busybody's identification hadn't been unexpected—it had—but this had the added kick of being the *reverse* of what I'd expected. Instead of exonerating me, Minton had stuck my neck in the noose.

But he'd done something else, too. And as soon as I got over the initial shock and calmed down somewhat, I realized what it was. He'd done the thing that I always need done for me in a case like this.

He'd told me who did it.

Minton was lying. Miss Busybody and the stupid secretary could have been mistaken, but not Minton. Minton was lying. And if Minton was lying, he had to have a reason. And the only reason that made any sense was that he was guilty. That he was the murderer.

So actually Minton had done me a favor.

Although, at the present time, I wasn't in any position to appreciate it.

All three men were looking at me.

"Well," Barnes said. "Do you have anything to say for yourself?"

"What do you mean?" I asked.

"Do you admit you hired this man?"

"Absolutely not."

"He says that you did."

"He's lying."

Barnes and Preston looked at each other. They shook their heads. Laughed.

"Sure," Barnes said. "He's lying. His secretary's lying. And Steerwell's next-door neighbor is lying."

"No," I said. "They're mistaken. He's lying."

"I see," Barnes said. "Everyone's wrong but you."

"That's right."

"And I suppose this entry in Minton's notebook is a mistake, too," Barnes said, with elaborate sarcasm. "He probably meant to write some other name, but accidentally wrote the name Stanley Hastings instead."

"May I see the notebook," I said.

"Why?"

"I'd just like to see it."

Barnes thought that over. "You can't touch it, but you can look."

He took the notebook from Minton, turned it around, and held it open for me to see.

"Just as I thought," I said.

"What?"

"It's a loose-leaf notebook."

"So what?"

"The pages are not dated."

"No. The dates are written in pen."

"Exactly."

"So what?"

"The page with my name on could have been written at any time. It could have come from the back of the notebook. Minton could have taken a page from the back, dated it, written my name on it, and then stuck it in the book in the proper sequence. It could have been done an hour ago."

Minton smiled, a cold, thin smile. "You don't quit, do you?"

"No I don't, Mr. Minton. Now you claim I came to your agency and hired you?"

"You know you did."

"Fine. And just what did I hire you to do?"

Minton smiled and shrugged. "I have no idea."

"What?!"

"You came to me and said you wanted to hire a private detective for a routine surveillance job. I told you my rates were two hundred dollars a day plus expenses. You griped about the price a good deal, but eventually you agreed to pay it. As soon as we'd agreed to terms, I assigned the case to Steerwell and turned you over to him to discuss the details." Minton turned to Barnes. "You understand, this was just routine. I no longer do my own legwork. I'm an administrator, and my main job is fixing fees. I have a number of operatives working for me, and I farm the work out to them on an hourly basis. In routine cases of this kind, I don't concern myself with the specifics of the case, I leave it to the operative, in this case, Steerwell. Of course, my operatives are well trained, and in the event a routine assignment should develop into something more, the operative would report to me, and if the situation warranted, then I would personally involve myself in the case. At least to the point of adjusting fees."

God, he was good. Smooth and oily enough to make your flesh crawl, but good.

"Are you trying to tell me," I said sarcastically, "that you go ahead and fix fees without knowing the specifics of a case?"

"Certainly not," Minton said. "If I might have my notebook back." He took it from Barnes and referred to it. "Now in your case, what you requested was a simple surveillance, one man, eight hours, in this case eight o'clock to four o'clock. It was a straight shadowing job, nonelectronic, no extras." He looked at me and smiled. "At least, that is what you kept stressing in the meeting when you were attempting to get me to reduce my fees. If you'll recall, as I told you, two hundred is a flat minimum, and all those things would have been extras, anyway."

"You son of a bitch," I murmured. It was as much in awe as in anger. God, he was cool.

Minton opened his mouth, but Barnes jumped in quickly. "I think that's all, Mr. Minton. You've been very cooperative, and I wouldn't want you to wind up getting into a squabble with the suspect. Why don't you leave us to sort these things out?"

"Certainly," Minton said. "If I can be of further assistance."

"We'll be in touch," Barnes said.

Preston stepped aside, and Minton went out the door. The cops watched him go, then turned to face me.

I wouldn't want you to get the impression I was getting any braver. The fact is, I was scared shitless.

FAVOR

Minton had left me up the creek without a paddle, and my chances of getting back down again appeared slim.

But the thing is, when you're totally fucked, you got nothing left to lose.

Which is why I couldn't resist.

I spread my arms wide, palms up, shrugged my shoulders, cocked my head, and smiled.

"Well," I said. "Here we are."

27

"Well, what do we do with him now?"

"That, of course, is the question," Barnes said.

"I guess we should talk it over."

"I suppose so."

"Do you suppose we should talk it over with him?"

"I don't know if he wants to talk to us."

"Well, he certainly wanted to talk to Minton."

"Yeah, well, that's only natural," Barnes said. "After all, he employed him. You always want to talk to the guy you hired. Find out if you made a good investment. If you're getting your money's worth. It doesn't mean he'll want to talk to us. He didn't employ us."

"Well, he's a taxpayer, isn't he?"

"Yeah, but he's from New York."

"That's true."

"So he probably won't talk to us."

"We could ask him."

"I suppose so."

"Does this mean we have to read him his rights again? I'm getting mighty sick of it."

"I'm getting mighty sick of it, too." Barnes turned to me. "Mr. Hastings, would you like to do us all a big favor and stipulate that your rights have been read? I'd hate to drag Preston through it again."

God, these guys were good. It was psychological torture of the worst kind. A third degree would have been a relief compared to it. Anything rather than their inane, jovial banter.

"All right, look, guys," I said. "I know you're having a good time. But frankly, this is a little hard for me to handle. I don't do murders. I do broken arms and legs. Then this thing comes along. The witnesses blow an identification and suddenly I'm a murder suspect. Then I have to wait a whole day for the guy to come who can get me off the hook. And then, for some reason that I cannot fathom, he screws me instead. Now, I would just love to play macho with you boys, and keep up the bright, snappy patter. But I happen to be a card-carrying coward, and the truth is, I'm on the verge of a nervous breakdown. So do whatever the hell it is you guys gotta do, because I am not the swiftest thinker in the world, and I have to adjust to being kicked in the face here."

Preston looked at Barnes.

"Emotional isn't he?"

"I'll say."

"It would appear we are going to have to continue this conversation without him."

"It would appear so."

"Why don't we do so, and then on the off chance his thought process should catch up with him, he can feel free to chime in."

"O.K.," Preston said. "So what have we got?"

Barnes shook his head. "Well, you know, it's a new one on me. The guy's been I.D.'d now by three independent witnesses. And yet he still maintains that he is innocent and these witnesses are either mistaken or lying. Now, aside from, say, Bennie Logan or petty thieves of his ilk, this doesn't happen. You don't have a moderately intelligent, educated person making a flat denial of that type. You see what I mean?"

"Yeah, I do. It's too stupid, even for him."

"Exactly. If an educated person were going to try to lie his way out of it, he would come up with something more convincing than an implausible flat denial."

"I agree."

"So why is he doing it?"

They both looked at me.

I said nothing. It wasn't a conscious decision on my part to say nothing. It was simply that by then my brain was Jell-O. I just gawked at them.

"O.K.," Barnes said. "Ridiculous as it sounds, let's suppose for a moment that this guy is telling the truth."

"I find that hard to swallow."

"So do I. But let's just take it as a premise. O.K., if this guy is telling the truth, what does it mean?"

"It means Minton is lying."

"That's one thing. Now, why would Minton lie?"

"Because he's mixed up in it, of course."

"Of course. Which would make sense. He is Steerwell's boss. And there are those pictures Steerwell took."

"The ones our friend here took."

"Allegedly took. Do be fair, Preston. But leave that for a while. What about the other witnesses?"

"What *about* 'em?"

"The other witnesses can't be lying. Well, the secretary could, because she works for Minton, but not the next-door neighbor. That's too much to swallow. Unless you can find some way to connect her with Minton. But once you connect her with Minton, you get her coincidentally living next to Steerwell, and—it's just too much, it's too much, forget it."

"I agree."

"So, if this guy is telling the truth, and those witnesses aren't lying, then it must be as he says. They're mistaken."

"I'm with you so far."

"O.K. Well, that gives us a nice little picture. Here's this guy, sitting here. He's not guilty. He presumably has nothing to hide. And yet he's a clam. He won't tell us anything. Why is that? Only one reason. He's protecting someone. Who? A client."

"Naturally."

"So, take it a step further. If the witnesses are mistaken, and he's protecting a client, then there's only one thing left that makes sense: the client that he's protecting is a man who looks enough like him to be mistaken for him, and that man is the man who hired Steerwell and the man who ran in and out of Steerwell's house."

Preston looked at me. "Anything to that, clam?"

I blinked. I opened my mouth, closed it again.

"He's not talking," Preston said.

"You really expect him to?" Barnes said.

"I suppose not."

"Well, that brings us back to the original problem. What do we do with him?"

"This is a problem," Preston said. "What do you think we should do?"

"I don't know," Barnes said. "I leave it up to you."

Jesus Christ. Here they were, playing dibbsies with my freedom as if they were discussing who went first in a game of marbles. And Barnes had just deferred to Preston, leaving my fate in Bad Cop's hands. Bad Cop would fry me.

Preston yawned and stretched. His hands brushed the ceiling. He looked like some giant bird, flexing its wings before swooping down on its prey.

He frowned and pursed his lips. "I say we let him go."

28

The revenge of Bad Cop.

They'd done it again. Preston had just one-upped me in the game of "You can go"—"Then I'll stay."

And this time I wasn't ready to go for the win by saying, "That's all right, let's talk." An incredulous, "Huh," was the best I could muster.

"That's interesting," Barnes said. "And now, why would you say that?"

Preston shrugged. "Well, the problem, you see, is motive. Now, I know we got the theft of the pictures, we got the fingerprints on the wallet and we got the three eyewitness identifications and all that. But the problem still is motive. I just can't fathom why a douche-bag ambulance chaser from New York City who's never been here before should come down here and kill two people. It just doesn't make any sense."

"Whereas the bit about protecting a client I can buy."

"You're saying you believe him?"

"Well, no, I'm not saying that. I'm just saying the explanation could be plausible. And, of course, we have to consider the alternatives."

"Such as?"

"Well," Preston said. "We've got enough to arrest him on suspicion of murder. We could hold him on that. But the prosecutor isn't going to be too happy. Because we don't have enough to convict. Because we don't have the motive. And we're not going to get it, 'cause the guy's a clam.

"And then we have practical matters to consider. If we arrest him for murder, then we gotta lock him up in the county jail way the fuck out in Mays Landing. And then we gotta run out there every time we wanna talk to him or have some witness I.D. him or whatever."

"Oh, you're always griping about the county jail in Mays Landing."

"Well, it's a real pain in the ass. I suppose you like going out there. And another thing is, if we charge him with murder, that asshole lawyer will come roaring back in that fucking stretch-limo and start screaming at everybody until we won't be able to think straight."

"I hope Mr. Hastings didn't misunderstand you," Barnes said. "What Sergeant Preston meant to say, was that he would certainly hate to inconvenience your estimable attorney by making him come all the way back from New York."

"Certainly," Preston said. "My sentiments exactly."

Barnes turned back to me. "Well, Mr. Hastings. I think Sergeant Preston's made a pretty good case. The only thing is, letting you go is going to get us some awfully bad press. I mean, what with there being so much evidence against you, and all. But we aren't out to win any popularity contests here. What we are concerned with is the administration of justice. A very corny thing to have to say, but there you are. The point is, we don't really give a shit what people say about us, as long as we're doing our job. We can take the flak."

Barnes looked at Preston, nodded, then looked back at me.

"So you can go."

29

This time I knew they were following me.

I didn't see them, of course. I'm no good at that. But I knew. It was the only thing that made sense. The only reason they could have released me this time. Oh, a lot of what Barnes and Preston had said was true. And a lot of what they surmised was deadly accurate. But still, I would have been willing to bet you that releasing me would not have turned out to be the prescribed course of action written in the police procedural. No, they had to have a reason.

They were following me for sure.

And if that was true, I had a lot to consider.

As I've said, I couldn't lead them to Harold and Barbara.

But where could I lead them?

I figured I had twenty-four, maybe forty-eight hours at the outside, before the whole thing blew up in my face. By then, one of a number of unpleasant things would have happened. The cops would have got a lead to Harold and Barbara. Or Barnes and Preston, for all their bravado, would take so much heat they'd have to pick me up and charge me.

Or I'd crack up.

The third possibility seemed the most likely. And it

wasn't necessarily going to take any twenty-four to forty-eight hours, either. If you can't understand that, then you probably (1) have never been arrested for murder and (2) are thinking of TV detectives who get arrested for murder every week and are used to it so it doesn't faze them.

Don't judge a man till you've been standing in his shoes. Madonna sings that in one of the songs on her *True Blue* album. Shit. Do I have to confess to listening to Madonna? Well, I'd rather do that than confess to murder. Why am I saying this? I've got confession on the brain. Why? I'm not guilty. At least not of murder. Grand larceny, well, that's another matter. God, how often can I say that? Yes, I'm guilty of grand larceny. How glamorous. I bet that could get me laid in the singles bars. "Hi, I'm guilty of grand larceny. Wanna fuck?" Jesus, what a line. No, I can't handle it. Maybe I should just confess. Confess to the murders, too. Then they'd leave me alone. Then I wouldn't have to think about it. Then—

Shit.

I *am* cracking up.

I lay in the bed in my hotel room, drenched with sweat and torn with doubts.

What the hell should I do?

I got up, took my clothes off and took a shower. When in doubt, take a shower.

When I got out, I felt cooler, if not more clear-headed. I put on fresh clothes and combed my hair. I looked at myself in the mirror. Damn it, I didn't look a thing like Harold Dunleavy. Not that I wanted to. As far as I was concerned, the only thing I envied about Harold Dunleavy was Barbara MacAullif Dunleavy.

Somehow I had to help her.

And him.

I picked up the phone and called MacAullif. I was hoping he might have some advice, seeing as how I was sort of at wit's ends, myself.

He was out. Just my luck. The one time I *wanted* to talk to him.

I called Alice. She was glad to hear from me. It had been a while. In all the excitement I'd forgotten to call home. I told her I'd been busy.

She asked me how the case was going. I told her things were coming along.

I shaded the truth a little. Alice asked me how I was, and I told her I was fine. I saw no reason to alarm her.

I didn't lie to her. I just didn't mention that I'd been indicted for grand larceny and was suspected of two murders.

A sin of omission.

I hung up the phone. I felt awful. I'd needed to talk to somebody. MacAullif wasn't there, and this was something I couldn't talk over with my wife.

I was on my own.

All right, asshole, what are you going to do?

I realized it didn't matter. I just had to do something, anything, or I'd go nuts.

I went out and got in my car. I pulled out of the parking lot, headed for Atlantic City. I didn't know where I was going, I was just going. That was the ticket. Don't think about it. Just do it.

I knew the cops were following me. It was amusing. I wondered what they'd think if they realized I didn't know where I was going.

The signs assaulted me again. The signs for the casinos. They were like sirens, calling to me. Luring me.

I succumbed to the lure.
Fuck it.
Let the cops follow me.
I'll lead 'em somewhere.
To the casino.
To Tallman.

30

Harold Dunleavy wasn't in Tallman's Casino. It wouldn't have mattered if he had been. The cops wouldn't have been able to single him out from the other few thousand people there. And he didn't know me, so there was no chance of him rushing up to me and saying, "Hey, you son of a bitch, what you doing messing around in this case?"

It would have been reassuring to see him, actually. Particularly since I couldn't risk driving by his house anymore. It would have been nice to know he hadn't skipped town. It also would have been nice to know that he was still alive. So many of the people I'd been following lately had been winding up dead. But Harold wasn't there.

M. Carson, the blonde, nimble-fingered blackjack dealer wasn't there, either.

Neither was Tallman, for that matter.

All in all, it looked like a pretty unprofitable evening. Well, I'd left the hotel with low expectations, so it wasn't that surprising to see them fulfilled.

One good thing: this would sure keep the boys from Major Crimes guessing.

I figured I'd hang out for a while and see if anyone showed up.

I dug the change out of my pocket. I had five quarters. Well. Big spender. What the hell.

I walked over to a slot machine and fed the quarters in one at a time.

On the fourth one I hit a ten-quarter payoff.

Hot damn.

I celebrated by playing two quarters at once.

I hit a twenty-quarter payoff. Right after that, another payoff for eight.

Jesus Christ. I was getting to where I could use one of those plastic cups.

I hit another twenty-quarter payoff.

Christ, I was smoking. At this rate, I might hit the jackpot. Two thousand quarters. Let's see, divide by four, that's five hundred dollars. I could imagine the phone call to my wife: "That's right, honey, I went in there with a buck twenty-five, and guess what?"

My last quarter came up zilch.

I smiled wistfully, returned my plastic cup to its former place.

I looked at my watch. My entire trip through exultation into bankruptcy had taken a whopping fifteen minutes.

I looked around. Still no sign of Harold and M. Carson. But some men that looked vaguely familiar were threading their way through the tables at the end of the room. As they drew closer, they dispelled all doubt. It was the King and his Court.

Well, fuck it. I wanted to lead the cops to Tallman, and there's Tallman. So what did I do now?

I felt like looking behind me, whistling, and pointing, "There he is!" Somehow that didn't strike me as being very wise. What I had to do was go up to him and speak to him. The thing was, I couldn't think of a fucking thing to say. You see, I didn't want to say anything that would be even remotely connected to the case.

That was largely because of the King's Court.

Now, I am admittedly not the best judge of character in the world, but it didn't take a genius to see that these guys were most likely not the King's financial advisors. In fact, if their average I.Q. was over a hundred, I'd have lost another bet.

I didn't know if Tallman was mob connected and these guys were mob, or if these guys were local talent he'd just hired himself, but either way, they looked like muscle, not brains. So, under the circumstances, murder didn't seem like a good subject to bring up.

So what was I gonna say? I didn't know. But I was winging it all the way, anyway, so what the hell.

I stepped away from the slot machine right into the path of a waitress with a tray of drinks. She stopped short, martinis and breasts both jiggling and threatening to escape the confines of their containment. She started to flash me a dirty look, then, apparently remembering the customer was always right, converted it into a lopsided smile, and skipped nimble-footedly around me.

I sidestepped too, then strode out into the middle of the floor and headed straight for Tallman.

As I approached, the hands of two of the members of the King's Court strayed inside their jackets. I wondered why. Then I realized. I was wearing a suit and tie, and so were they, and so was almost no one else in the casino. After all, it was Atlantic City in the summertime. Short sleeve shirts were the order of the day.

I tried not to notice the hands in the jackets. I strode right up to Tallman.

"Hey, Tallman," I said. "I've got a bone to pick with you."

The Court tensed.

The King afforded me a regal, condescending look.
"Oh?"

"Yeah. These waitresses you got working here. In
the skimpy costumes with the boobs pushed up and
jiggling like Jell-O. That's bullshit, man. That's bush
league. I come in here after a hard day's work. I'm
gambling, I'm dropping some money. You think I
want to see that shit? All tease and titillation? I can
get that on TV. You think I want to see push-up
costumes? Hell no! Bare breasts, that's what I want to
see. Bare tits."

One of the King's Court took a step forward.

"You want I should get rid of this bird?"

The King raised his hand and stopped him.

"No. Let him talk. The guy has a point."

Good lord. The man was a total moron. *I* had a
point.

"Damn right I got a point," I said. "And it's a big
one. In fact, it's two big ones. I'm talkin' boobs. Jugs.
Hooters. Look at the flight deck on that waitress over
there. That's something huh? But the damn costume. I
don't want to see fabric, I want to see flesh. Topless
waitresses, that's what I'm talkin' here. Look, you go
to any casino on the strip, and you see the same thing.
Friggin' Playboy bunny costumes. You can be different. The King of the bare boobs. You'll pack 'em in."

Tallman nodded. "I'll think about it," he said.

Then he and his entourage moved off.

It was great. It was so great. There couldn't have
been a cop close enough to hear what I was saying.
But they were there all right. They could see me. They
could see me talking to the King. And they could
see me shoving my finger in his face and making my
points. And they could see his boys starting to move

on me, and the King stopping them with his regal gesture. And then the King nodding and moving off.

What would Barnes and Preston make of all that?

I went back to the garage, got in my car and assessed my performance. I realized my rap to Tallman had been both puerile and manic, but that didn't matter.

It had also been fun.

I realized I shouldn't be having fun. I was in probably the worst fix of my life, and my chances of getting out of it were incredibly slim. The fact I was having fun meant only one thing: I was over the edge. I'd lost it. I'd snapped.

But that didn't stop me from having it. Hey, life was a ball.

So what should I do now, I thought? I had no idea. But I realized it didn't matter. Whatever I did, the cops would go with me. Follow the leader. And I got to lead. What fun.

It was a merry chase.

31

"**M**inton."

I was calling on an old friend. I figured, hell, if I was having fun, it was time to renew old acquaintance.

Sallingsworth inspected the bottle of bourbon.

"You want a lot for a pint of whiskey."

"Hey," I said. "Give me a break. It's not like I'm the worst thing that ever happened to you. I mean, think about it. A private dick comes down from New York, you think, 'Shit, more competition. Someone else gonna take away more of my business.' But what do I do? I bring you business. I bring you business and I bring you bourbon. What's more, I eliminate the competition. Hey, Steerwell's dead, ain't he? Give me a little ammunition to shoot and I'll take down Minton. It won't be long before you'll be the only game in town."

Sallingsworth cocked his head and looked at me narrowly.

"Are you all right?"

"I wouldn't think so. I have two murder raps hanging over my head, not to mention one grand larceny."

"That's not what I mean. You're acting rather strange."

"That's only because I've lost my grip on reality. Aside from that, I'm fine."

Sallingsworth looked at me as if he'd just I.D.'d the escaped psycho half the county had been looking for.

"I see," he said.

"Aw, drink up, drink up," I told him. "Whether you talk to me or not, the bourbon's yours. I don't drink the stuff, and I'm certainly not taking it back. So go ahead. Knock yourself out."

Sallingsworth broke the seal and opened the bottle. He took a pull from the neck. He wasn't standing on ceremony enough to bother getting a glass. He also wasn't leaving this lunatic alone in the room.

"That's better," I said. "Now tell me about Minton. He's a fine man. You've always admired him. When he was coming up in the business, you said, 'Hey, this one's gonna be tops.' "

Sallingsworth looked at me. "Jesus Christ," he said. He took another pull from the bottle.

"Hey," I said. "No one's quoting you on this. I'm not doing an article for *True Detective*. And I'm not running to Minton to tattle. He won't be showing up here tomorrow saying, 'Hey, you told that New York dick I was a dipshit.' It's just you and me having a little chat."

He took another pull from the bottle. Looked at me thoughtfully.

"It's getting to you, isn't it," he said. "You're really cracking up, aren't you?"

I looked back at him. "Well, wouldn't you?"

"So Minton I.D.'d you as the murderer."

"He had to. It was his civic duty."

Sallingsworth grunted. "Yeah." He took another drink. "All right," he said. "I'll give you all I've got, for all it's worth. Minton's a sleaze. He's scum. He's the type of private detective that gives us all a bad name. He cuts corners. He lies. He cheats. He fakes evidence. He rips off his own clients. He pads bills. He bills for summonses not served, surveillance not performed."

Sallingsworth took another pull, wiped his mouth with the back of his hand. "I did a lot of business in this town before that slime showed up. He muscled me out of there. Undercut me. Bad-mouthed me. That was when he used to do his own work. Now he has operatives. He's just a bookkeeper, he just skims off the top. He still cuts corners, chisels, cheats on fees."

He stopped, looked at me. "But you know all that, don't you? Or if you don't, it's old news, and you don't care. It's not what you're after. You just need something that's gonna help you now."

He took another pull on the bottle. His eyes gleamed—craftily.

"Well, there's one thing. And I'll bet you I'm the only guy who knows it. Because it goes way back, and not too many people knew it then. But when Minton first started out, he did a lot of different things, 'cause he was hustling, trying to get going. He had a lot of irons in the fire. God, I could tell you stories. But then you wouldn't be interested.

"Except for one thing." Sallingsworth leaned back and cocked his head at me. "Now you have to remember, this was a long time ago. So maybe it helps you and maybe it don't. But here it is."

He took a long pull on the bottle, and looked at me.

"He used to work with Nubar."

32

I had one more person I didn't mind leading the cops to. I mean, it wasn't the best of all possible worlds, but it wasn't a total disaster, either.

Up to now I'd been pretty frustrated by having been barred from talking to any of the principles in this case. I mean Sallingsworth was a nice guy and all that, but he was peripheral at best. I sure as hell wanted to talk to somebody else.

Of course, I still couldn't talk to the person I wanted to talk to most. That, of course, being Barbara MacAullif Dunleavy. So I had to settle for second best.

I cruised by her apartment house. If Harold Dunleavy's car had been parked outside I would have had to keep on going, but it wasn't. I stopped my car and got out.

I went up the steps and went inside. The foyer door was open, as it had been the time before. I went up the stairs, found the apartment and rang the bell.

There was a long pause, then footsteps, and the door opened a crack. I could see half a face looking out at me.

"M. Carson?" I said.

I gave her my best steely-eyed gaze. I'm sure it

looked ridiculous, and anyone who knew me would have been on the floor laughing.

But M. Carson didn't know me.

"Yes," she said uncertainly.

"Homicide," I said and pushed the door open.

M. Carson fell back in alarm.

I pushed by her and walked into the living room.

She closed the front door and trailed in behind me. She looked utterly dazed.

M. Carson was dressed in a negligee with a flimsy robe thrown over it. I guess she'd been in bed, which she had every right to be. By then it was one in the morning. She looked good. Not in Barbara Dunleavy's class, but good.

"I'm sorry to bother you," I said, "but we're cleaning up these two murders and we have to tie up all loose ends."

"How . . . How did you find me?" she asked.

I smiled a cold, superior smile. Again, friends would have been amused.

"I . . . I . . ." she began. "Won't you sit down?"

"Thanks," I said.

I sat in the easy chair.

"Can I get you a drink?"

"No. You sit down."

She sat on the couch opposite me.

"You're stalling for time," I said, "wondering how bad this is. Well, on the one hand, it's pretty bad. On the other hand, it's not as bad as you think. If it was, you'd be on your way downtown."

She looked at me and bit her lip.

"You still could wind up there," I said. "You're not a principal, so it's up to you. This is your chance to come clean."

"I don't know what you're talking about," she said.

I shook my head.

"That's the wrong way to play it. I'll tell you what I'm talking about so there'll be no mistake. Then it's up to you. If you want to go down swinging, that's fine, but it don't have to be that way.

"All right, here it is. Minton killed Nubar. He also killed Steerwell. He set up a phony alibi of going to Vegas that's as old as the hills. He went there all right, then had some private plane fly him back. We haven't traced the plane yet, but we will."

Her eyes were wide. "What are you saying?"

"I haven't said anything yet, but I'm about to. This is the part you're not going to like. See, it's all about Tallman."

Her eyes flicked.

"Yeah, that's right, Tallman. See why this concerns you? Tallman isn't mob connected. He'd like you to think he is, but that's a bunch of bullshit. He was always a fast-talking confidence man, getting by on a shoe-shine and a smile. Tallman was in deep to Nubar. Real deep. It was the only way he could get off the ground and stay afloat. It was a secret. A big one. If anybody knew that, his whole empire would have collapsed. You knew it, but damn few people did.

"But Minton knew. He made it his business to know. That's how he's always made his living. That's the kind of creep he is. And as soon as he found out, he moved in. Not on Nubar, of course. He moved in on Tallman.

"But Minton wasn't your typical shakedown artist. There was nothing small-time about him. He didn't want a few grand here, a few grand there. He wanted a piece of the action.

"So he became a partner. A silent partner. That was O.K. with Tallman, because, frankly, he needed the help. And the thing he needed help with was Nubar.

"Minton knew Nubar, and one thing he knew was,

189

no one ever wriggles off Nubar's hook. Even with the fantastic amounts Tallman's Casino was pulling down, there was no way out. Nubar's interest was back-breaking, as it always was. So what was the upshot? Tallman and Minton wound up busting their balls working their butts off for Nubar.

"There was only one way out. Get rid of Nubar.

"Tallman, for all his bluster, didn't have the guts to do it, but not Minton. Minton was a cold-blooded son of a bitch. He set the thing up. He'd fly to Vegas, get a friendly pilot to fly him back, bump off Nubar and that would be that.

"Then something happened to queer the pitch.

"Steerwell.

"Steerwell found out the connection between Tallman and Nubar. Steerwell wanted in. That didn't suit Minton's plans at all. So he decided to clear up Steerwell at the same time he took care of Nubar.

"There was just one thing. There had to be a fall guy. And that's where Harold Dunleavy comes into all this, and that's why it involves you."

She sprang up from the couch.

"No, no! It wasn't like that at all!"

I could have kissed her. I'd been going on and on, making up bullshit off the top of my head, just waiting for her to jump in and contradict me, and I was just about running out of steam. If she hadn't come in then, I was very close to grinding to halt, in which case I probably would have just stood there like an asshole, like an actor who's dried up and forgot his lines. I might have even broken down and started crying, which probably would have given the show away. So I was mighty glad she chimed in.

"The hell it wasn't," I said. "You had Dunleavy all groomed to take the rap. Then the witnesses blew the identification and named the wrong man. That threw

Minton for a loop. He didn't dare name Dunleavy then. So he hopped on the bandwagon and named the other guy, too, figuring one fall guy's as good as another. So Dunleavy escaped, no thanks to you. If everything had gone as planned, Dunleavy would have taken the rap, and Dunleavy would have gone down."

Her eyes were wide.

"No, no, you can't pin that on me. It was just a coincidence."

"I don't believe in coincidence," I said. I was pleased with myself. It was what MacAullif would have said.

"You don't understand. You've got it all wrong."

"Then why don't you straighten me out?"

"And if I do?"

"We're after the big fish here. If you cooperate, you'll walk. If you don't, there's no guarantees."

She bit her lip.

"O.K., listen. You have to believe me. I didn't know anything about this. I didn't know what they were planning. The murders, I mean. It was a shock to me. I didn't even know Nubar was dead until I heard it on the radio."

"Go on."

"I tell you, I know nothing about the murders. You tell me Minton did it, well, I can believe that, it makes sense, but I know nothing about it."

"You know enough about it to tell me Dunleavy wasn't groomed as a patsy."

"But he wasn't. It was just coincidence."

"That Dunleavy hired Steerwell? I can't buy that."

She shook her head. "No, no. That wasn't coincidence. That was . . . Ah, hell!"

"You're not helping yourself any."

A tear rolled down her cheek. She brushed it away. Looked around. She looked like some trapped wild animal. I would have liked to have felt sorry for her, but I can't say that I did.

"Harold Dunleavy," I said.

She snuffled. "Yeah?"

"You say he wasn't a patsy. Then what was he?"

There was a box of tissues on the table by the end of the couch. She pulled a couple out and blew her nose. She sank back down on the couch.

"It was all Tallman's idea," she said.

"What's Tallman to you?"

She shot me a hard look. "What do *you* think?"

I nodded. "Go on. What was all Tallman's idea?"

"The thing with Harold Dunleavy. You gotta understand about that. Harold Dunleavy had some debts. Big debts. He was in hock to Nubar. And Tallman was in hock to Nubar. *That* was the coincidence. It's not really that much of a coincidence, either. In this town, if you have big debts, you're in hock to Nubar."

She drew her legs up on the couch. Green as I am at this game, I recognized the action. She'd resigned herself to talking now, and she was getting expansive and settling in.

"The thing about Harold Dunleavy is, he's one of those little guys who like to talk big. He's a stockbroker, you know that? I gather he's not that important in his firm, but to hear him talk, you'd think he was the executive vice-president. He drives a flashy car he can't afford that's financed to the hilt. You must know the type."

I nodded. "But what's this got to do with Tallman?"

"Tallman's much the same way, but on a larger scale. Everything I said about Dunleavy goes ten times for Tallman. But you know all that. You know Tallman was into Nubar and that whole story. At any rate, Harold met Ray, and—"

"Who?"

She flushed. "I'm sorry. Tallman. Ray Tallman."

She seemed embarrassed by the intimacy, and I figured she'd make a conscious effort to use Tallman's last name from here on.

She did.

"Dunleavy met Tallman," she said. "Not through Nubar. Through the casino. See, Harold's a gambler. That's how he got into all this trouble in the first place. He's a bad gambler. A plunger. One of those guys who thinks he's a high roller, but's really a fish.

"But he talks a good line, you know. And anyway, he got to talking to Tallman, and he's coming off with this I'm-a-big-stockbroker bullshit. And he's handing Tallman a line and kidding him along, and trying to get him to advance him some credit at the casino.

"So Dunleavy's mouthing off and telling Tallman, because he's a stockbroker he has this connection in New York who is feeding him information about a couple of big corporate mergers that he's gonna act on, and inside of twelve to eighteen months he'll be rolling in dough. And Tallman, who is desperate for dough and needs some sort of big score to get out from under Nubar, is eating it up.

"So Tallman's trying to get Dunleavy to open up and let him in on this big thing. And Dunleavy's just smiling and shaking his head, no way. That's when Tallman told me to work on Dunleavy."

I looked at her. "So it *was* insider trading."

She looked at me. "What, are you nuts? Insider trading? What insider trading? There was no insider trading. There were no big corporate mergers. Dunleavy was just shooting off his mouth, like I said. I tried to tell Tallman that. He wouldn't listen. He was after the big score."

"So what happened?"

"What do you think happened? I made a play for

Dunleavy, and he fell for me hard. But he wouldn't tell me anything about this big insider score, which was natural enough, seeing as how there was nothing to tell.

"I told this to Tallman. He wouldn't listen. He said, 'Bullshit, he's holding out on you.' "

She looked at me. "Tallman's not very bright."

"I'll buy that. Go on."

"Well, he wouldn't give up. He says Dunleavy's holding out on me because he thinks I'm working for him. For Tallman, I mean. I gotta relax him, make him feel good, make him think I'm on his side."

She stopped. Took a breath. Looked at me.

"So he tells me to cheat for him."

"You're kidding."

"I'm not. Look, I'm a blackjack dealer, and a good one. And I know how to stack a deck. I know how to cheat. Most of Tallman's dealers do. 'Cause he's desperate for money, see? And we have orders, if there's a chance of some guy making a big run on the bank, to knock him back, you know what I mean?

"But this time Tallman tells me to cheat the other way. To cheat for Dunleavy." She raised her eyebrows ironically. "Because of his *big* stock-trading score. So he says, 'Cheat for him. Let him win money to pay back Nubar. Cheat for him big, just so it don't go over ten thousand a night.' "

"How could you do that?"

"Easy. I worked it out with Dunleavy. I stacked the deck according to how many players there were at the table. The indicator was the last card dealt the previous time through the deck. Any time that came up as the last card dealt in a hand, it meant Dunleavy would win the next hand."

"What was to stop Dunleavy from breaking the bank?"

"Two things. One, the indicator was only gonna come up right every five or six times through the deck. And then Tallman had me report exactly how much Dunleavy won. He'd pass the information on to Nubar, so Nubar'd be sure to take most of it and only leave him with a small stake, so he'd have to work his way up again. Of course, Dunleavy knew that Nubar had a spy in the casino. He just never knew it was me."

"And how did Dunleavy come to hire Steerwell? You say it wasn't a set-up. Well, that's the coincidence I don't buy."

"It wasn't a coincidence. And it wasn't a set-up, either. At least, I don't think it was. I'll tell you how it happened. See, Dunleavy fell for me hard, of course." She smiled. "That's not being conceited. You throw a guy a girl *and* ten grand a night, and he's gonna fall hard.

"But the thing is, he was hooked bad. I didn't want to encourage him, but I couldn't *dis*courage him, either. Not with Tallman egging me on. So anyway, Harold went overboard. Sold himself on the idea of dumping his wife and taking up with me. Except, what with me in the picture, Harold figured his wife's lawyers would take him to the cleaners. He was pretty sure she had some outside interests and he wanted to get the goods on her, you know, so when the lawyers started haggling, it would be tit for tat. So he told me he was going to hire a private detective.

"That's when I went to Tallman and told him this thing was going too far, and it had to stop. I mean, I wasn't going through a marriage ceremony with this guy. Believe me, I was really upset.

"Tallman told me to calm down, it wouldn't be that much longer, just kid the guy along.

"Anyway, Tallman figured if Dunleavy wanted to hire a private detective, fine, let him do it. Only he didn't like the idea of Harold taking anyone into his confidence, even on a small thing like that. And he wanted to keep tabs on him.

"So he told me to send him to Minton."

My eyes widened. "So *that's* why Dunleavy hired Steerwell."

"That's right. And it wasn't a set-up. At least, I don't think it was. I don't know anything about the murders. I didn't know they were gonna happen, you see."

"But you knew after."

"What do you mean?"

"When you heard about the murders. You knew what had happened. You knew who'd done it."

She was shaking her head back and forth. "No, no. You have to believe me. I didn't know. There was no way I could know. It makes sense now, when you tell me about it. Only—"

"Only what?"

"Well, you're all wet about some of it."

"Oh, yeah? Like what?"

"Like the bit about Minton being Tallman's partner."

"He wasn't?"

"Hell, no. Why would Minton want to hook up with Tallman? The casino was in deep hock to Nubar. You don't jump on a sinking ship. Minton was putting the bite on him, that's all."

I frowned. "Wait a minute. That doesn't make any sense."

"What?"

"You said Tallman told you to send Dunleavy to Minton."

"Right."

"Why would he do that if Minton was putting the bite on him?"

"Yeah. That surprised me, too. I asked him. Tallman

said he and Minton had made a deal. At the time I didn't know what the deal was. Now I do."

"What?"

"What you said. A partnership. *If* Minton took care of Nubar."

"How do you know that?"

"I don't. It's just the only thing that makes sense. Minton was squeezing Tallman. Nubar was squeezing Tallman. Tallman made a deal with Minton. You tell me Minton killed Nubar. If that's true, it all makes sense. With Nubar out of the way, the casino's a gold mine. So that had to be the deal. Minton leveraged himself a partnership with Tallman in return for taking care of Nubar."

I thought that over. It sounded good to me. Of course, by then my mind was mush and anything would have sounded good to me, but even so I figured she was probably right.

"All right," I said. "Let's get back to Harold Dunleavy."

"What about him?"

"Have you seen him since the murders?"

"Yeah. He was in there that night. I didn't talk to him then, of course. We never spoke to each other in the casino. Just dealer and customer.

"He was pretty cool, all things considered, but I could tell he was pretty shaken. I didn't know about the murders then, so I didn't know what was wrong. But I knew it was something. He just wasn't himself. He missed a couple of key cards and blew a couple of big bets. It wasn't like him. Sometimes I'd fuck up the deal and blow it for him—it's hard to stack the bottom of the deck, believe me—but not Harold. He'd be pissed as hell when that happened.

"Except that night. He kept making mistakes. Later

that night I found out why. He'd gone out to Steerwell's, walked in and found him dead."

"He told you that?"

"Sure he did. But the thing was, he didn't know about Nubar. He didn't find out till we heard it on the news. He was furious with himself. Actually, he was more scared at what Nubar was gonna do to him for not winning enough money than he was about finding Steerwell's body.

"It came on the news. We'd been listening to the radio, listening to the description of the man who ran in and out of Steerwell's house. And Harold's sitting there shaking in his boots, figuring the cops are gonna I.D. him. And then the news about Nubar came on.

"It was a shock, but it was a big relief, too. It actually calmed Harold down."

"How come he went out to Steerwell's?"

"What's the difference?"

"Big difference. It's the difference between whether he was set up or he just stumbled into it."

"I see. Well, Harold called Minton's agency looking for Steerwell and spoke to the secretary there."

"He give his name?"

"No."

"Go on."

"The secretary said Steerwell wasn't there and wasn't coming in. Harold asked how come, and the secretary, who must be dumb as a board, tells him. She says Steerwell called in that morning about some pictures that got lost. I mean, isn't that a hell of a thing to tell a client? So Harold gets hysterical, 'cause he figures they're pictures Steerwell took for him. So he pumps the secretary for information, and like a dope she gives it to him. She says Steerwell called in early in the morning hysterical because somebody else picked up his pictures at the Photomat, and he wants to know where the hell they are. The secretary looks around and can't find them, and the guy who signed for the pictures doesn't even work there. So the secretary decides the pictures have been stolen and she files a complaint with the police, even though Steerwell tells her not to. He didn't want the police to have anything to do with it.

"Of course, that makes Harold even more hysterical. He doesn't want the police to have anything to do with it any more than Steerwell. So he worms Steerwell's address out of this secretary and goes out there and finds him dead."

She paused. Looked at me. "Now you know as much about it as I do."

I thought that over. "I see," I said. "Harold wasn't the fall guy. He just blundered into it."

"That's right," she said. "See. I didn't set him up. I *didn't*. You gotta believe me."

"Where's Harold now?"

"Home, probably. I told him to stay away, to lie low, until all this blows over. It didn't take that much convincing. The guy's pretty scared."

"I would imagine." I rubbed my head. "All right. Tell me something."

"What?"

"About Harold Dunleavy."

"What about him?"

"You spent a lot of time with him, right?"

"Yeah. So?"

"So what did you think of him?"

She stared at me. "Hey. I told you. Tallman told me to work on him."

"I know. But aside from that. What was he like?"

"Why do you want to know?"

"I just do. Humor me."

I could tell she thought it was a stupid question. But she wasn't going to argue with a homicide cop.

"Well, it's like I told you. Harold's a little guy trying to be a big guy. That's his whole thing. That's what he saw in me, basically. A chance to be a big shot. But he's not. And he never will be. You know why? Because he doesn't have the stuff. He's not ruthless enough, you know what I mean?"

"Give me an example."

"Well, like hiring Steerwell."

"What about it?"

"Well, when he hired him, there he was coming off with this big 'I'm going to get the goods on my wife' shit, you know? But at the same time, I could tell he was afraid Steerwell really *would* find out something about his wife. And he didn't want that. Some guys are funny that way, you know?"

I knew.

And it was the best news I'd heard all day.

She looked at me with pleading eyes.

"Now look. I told you all I know. I swear it. I had nothing to do with these murders. So what's going to happen to me?"

I leaned back in my chair. "Let me think a minute." I looked at her. "Where you from?"

"Salt Lake City."

"How long you been out here?"

"A year and a half."

"Got any friends back there?"

She blinked her eyes. "Yeah," she said. "Yeah, I do." There was a wistful quality in her voice. "There was a guy back there. A nice guy. He was pretty strong for me. Sometimes I wonder if he still is."

"It might be a good time to find out."

She stared at me. "What are you saying?"

"All right, look," I said. "I'm not a cop. I'm private. But everything else I told you is true. This case is busting wide open and those guys are going down. You can either go with 'em or you can get out. If I were you, I'd get out."

"Who are you?" she said.

"I'm the guy the witnesses I.D.'d. The guy they took for Dunleavy."

"You don't look a thing like him."

"I'm glad to hear it. I happen to be a private detective working on the case. But it so happens I'm sick of being a murder suspect, so everything is coming down. Before it does, I'm advising you to get out.

"Now look, there's cops following me, so they'll know I've come here, but that's it. It's the middle of the night, they won't have that many men on the job. They'll take note of you, but they won't put a tail on you till tomorrow. They won't have the manpower. I figure you got a couple of hours at least.

"So, you got any money?"

"Yeah. I got some."

"All right, pack your bags and get out. Start packing now. I'll leave here and lead the cops on a chase and give you time to get away. Anything you can take with you, take. Anything you can't, leave. Don't have anything shipped. Don't leave a trace. Don't travel under your right name.

"What *is* your right name, by the way?"

That startled her. "It's Margery."

"All right, Margery, it's nice to meet you, now get out."

She stood up and stared at me. "Why are you doing this?"

"I'm a sucker for a pretty face. Never mind. Just go."

"But my life here."

"Yeah. Some kind of life. Listen, after guys like

Dunleavy and Tallman, that guy in Salt Lake City's gonna look awful good."

I got up and went to the door. She followed me.

"Fifteen minutes, no longer," I said. "Then you go."

She put her hand on my shoulder. Her eyes were misted over. "You're pretty wonderful, you know that?" she said.

I smiled and chucked her under the chin. I was doing Bogart. I almost said, "Here's lookin' at you, kid."

I didn't. What I said was, "I sure wish you could tell that to a homicide cop named Barnes."

33

It's great when you've lost your mind. When you're so far over the edge that what you do doesn't seem to matter anymore. And it's a good thing I had lost it, because, as I said, I'm a devout coward, and the things I was about to do were things I wouldn't normally have done.

Maybe that's not true. 'Cause somehow I always manage to do the things I have to do. Like on the job for Richard, when sometimes I have to go into some rundown project next to a Methadone clinic with a bunch of junkies hanging out all over the place. And me, a white man in a suit and tie, the only one in the area, standing out like a sore thumb, looking like a cop or an easy mark.

It isn't sane to go in there, but I have to, so I do. And I don't psych myself up to do it. I don't say, "Fuck it, you're Stanley Hastings, private detective, now get in there and kick some ass." I just go in there scared out of my mind and do it because I have to.

And in the end, that's what it comes down to: you just do it because you have to.

And the things I did in Atlantic City, I did because I had to, whether I was in my right mind or not.

Now, you might argue I had to be out of my mind to

let Margery Carson go. But that was actually one of the sanest things I did. The thing was, she could have got me off the hook with the cops. She could have told the cops I wasn't the guy who hired Steerwell. That would have branded Minton's identification as false and made him a liar. Then the identifications of Miss Busybody and the secretary would have collapsed as well.

That would have got me out of it, but it would have got Harold Dunleavy right into it. And, of course, in spite of everything, I was still obeying the prime directive. Getting her out of there was not only protecting Harold Dunleavy from the cops, it was removing Harold Dunleavy's prime source of temptation, which could go a long way toward settling his marital woes. Not that the Dunleavys necessarily had any marriage left to patch up, but if they did, it couldn't hurt.

The other thing was, situations change. Circumstances alter. You have to roll with the punches. Go with the flow. Adjust your parameters and full speed ahead.

Yeah, Margery Carson probably could have done a pretty good job of convincing the police I hadn't hired Steerwell.

But you see, the thing was, by that time I had decided that, all things considered, I probably *had* hired Steerwell.

34

"**I**'m here to settle my bill."

The dumb secretary at Minton's stared at me as if she'd seen a ghost. I couldn't blame her. After all, here I was. The murderer. The one that she'd I.D.'d. Standing there in front of her, large as life. Probably hell-bent on revenge.

"What?" she croaked.

"My name's Stanley Hastings and I've come to pay my bill. Can I have it, please?"

"I . . . I . . ."

"I haven't got all day, you know. Do you handle the bookkeeping or don't you?"

"I . . . I . . . Well, Mr. Minton, you see . . ."

"Fine. Then I'd better talk to Minton."

"Yes . . . well . . ."

The secretary gulped twice and dove for the phone. She hit the intercom button. "Mr. Minton . . . Sorry to bother you, sir. There's a gentleman here insists on paying his bill . . . That's right. A Mr. Stanley Hastings . . . Yes, sir."

The secretary hung up the phone and looked at me sideways. I've heard of someone looking at someone sideways before, but she took the cake. I swear she gave me a straight profile.

"Go right in," she said.

I stepped around the desk, pushed the door open and went in.

Minton was seated at his desk. I could see that the top drawer was open. I assumed that there was a gun in it. If so, it meant Minton had seen the same old movies I had.

"And what can I do for you, Mr. Hastings?" Minton said.

"I'm here to pay my bill."

"What bill?"

"You ought to know. The one you told the cops about. The bill for hiring Steerwell."

"Really?" Minton said. "I thought you told the cops you *didn't* hire Steerwell."

I smiled. "Yes, but one doesn't always tell the cops the truth, now does one, Mr. Minton?"

Minton furrowed his brow. "I'm not sure I understand this. You are now—pardon me if I use the word—admitting that you hired Steerwell?"

"Of course I hired Steerwell. Your secretary says I hired Steerwell. You say I hired Steerwell. Don't you think I'd be a damn fool to try to deny I hired Steerwell? All right. I hired him, and I'm here to pay the bill."

Minton looked at me narrowly. "I'm not sure I understand. No, I take that back. I'm *certain* I don't understand."

"It's perfectly simple. I'm admitting I hired Steerwell and I want to pay the bill."

"Why?"

"Ah! That's something else again. Good point, Mr. Minton. Why? Well, I'll tell you why. I happen to have a felony count of grand larceny pending against me for stealing Steerwell's photographs. Now, what I think you and the police and everyone else in this case have lost sight of, is the fact that if I hired Steerwell, then he took those pictures for *me*. They are *my* photographs. And I didn't steal them, because they

206

were rightfully mine to begin with. And the felony count disappears."

Minton looked at me.

"Son of a bitch," he murmured.

"Of course, that leaves two unanswered murder counts kicking around. But *I* haven't been charged with them yet, as evidenced by the fact that I am out here walking around."

"Son of a bitch," Minton said again.

"So," I said, "unless you're gonna wanna retract your identification of me as the person who hired Steerwell, you're gonna find yourself having one hell of a time trying to press a charge against me for the theft of those photographs."

"Son of a bitch," Minton murmured.

"I think you're getting into a rut," I told him. "Would you like to try something else?"

Minton looked at me. "You're admitting you stole those photographs?"

"Admitting? What's admitting? I'm just telling you I had a legal right to them."

"All right. But you're saying you have them."

"Of course."

Minton's face hardened.

"I want those photographs."

"I thought you might. So, we have a situation here, don't we? If I hired Steerwell, those photographs are mine, I'm gonna keep 'em, and I'm here to pay my bill.

"If I didn't hire Steerwell, those photographs aren't mine, and you just might get 'em back."

"You're saying if I go to the police—"

"I'm not saying shit, and you're not going to the police. I'm not saying anything. Any way you want to play it, the fact is I have those pictures, and if you want 'em, you're gonna have to pay."

He looked at me. "How much?"

"Now you're talkin'," I said. "When I got ahold of those pictures, they were worth twenty thousand dollars."

"Twenty thousand dollars!" Minton said.

"Yeah," I said. "But that was just when I got ahold of 'em. Now they're worth a hundred thousand."

"What!?" Minton said.

"You see," I said. "They're pictures of Tallman and Nubar together. Now you know what that means. They would have been disastrous to Tallman's empire. That's why I say they would have been worth twenty thousand dollars.

"But that was then, and this is now, as the Monkees would say. You ever used to watch the Monkees?"

He looked at me. "What?"

"It used to bother me that they didn't play their own instruments, but in retrospect they're great."

"What are you talking about?"

"Skip it. The fact is, the price of those photographs has gone up. 'Cause now they're evidence of murder."

Minton wet his lips.

"You don't know what you're saying."

"I don't? I'll give you till tonight to get a hundred thousand dollars together. If you get it, you get the pictures. If you don't, they go to the cops. I'm sorry to be so abrupt about it, but I'm getting really sick of being framed for murder."

I turned to go.

"But wait," he began.

I turned back.

"I'll call you. I'll tell you where. You just get the money."

I turned my back and walked out.

35

The King was walking the floor with his Court when I strode up to him. He recognized me and raised his hand.

"Hey," he said. "You know, I been thinking over your proposition."

"Is that so?" I said. "In that case, you're a jerk. I happen to be a private detective investigating the Steerwell and Nubar murders. Before you sic your goons on me, I think you should know I already talked to Minton and he's agreed to buy back the embarrassing pictures of you and Frederick Nubar. If anything should happen to me before then, those pictures will be delivered to the police. I know it's a corny old bit, but the thing is, it works.

"But I was glad to find out you share my enthusiasm for the female anatomy. You're my kind of guy."

I smiled, shot my finger at him and walked out.

In retrospect, I don't think my meeting with Tallman accomplished a damn thing in terms of my investigation.

But it sure was fun.

36

I had a great afternoon. It was great because I knew
the cops were following me. I didn't really see 'em,
although once I spotted a car that pulled away from the
curb right after I did, but it was probably nothing,
because I never saw it again.

But I knew they were there.

And you have no idea what a tremendous sense of
power that gave me. I was living poison. I was the kiss
of death. I could fuck up anybody in town I wanted
just by walking up and talking to 'em. "Excuse me,
sir, would you like to be a murder suspect? Why don't
you just chat with me for a minute?" "Excuse me,
ma'am, do you know what time it is? Thank you very
much, you're a murder suspect."

I stopped in a restaurant on Atlantic Avenue and
bought a cheeseburger. I overtipped the guy at the
counter, knowing I'd just sicced the cops on his case. I
hoped he had no health code violations.

I went out, got in my car and drove off. I kept
watch in my rearview mirror just in case anyone was
tagging along, but I couldn't spot 'em. Except for that
one time, and I might have imagined that.

I drove out on Ventnor Avenue to pick a place for
my meeting with Minton. I figured it had to be outside

so the cops would have a chance to move in. There was no way I wanted to wind up alone in a room with the guy.

I was nearly out to Steerwell's when I spotted an alley in the middle of a block. It looked pretty good. I stopped the car, got out, crossed Ventnor, and checked it out.

It was perfect. No illumination of any kind that I could see, except what would filter down from the street. Lots of doorways and alcoves that would become dark hiding places at night, for the cops to settle into.

I walked all the way up and down the alley, just to make sure the cops took the hint. Then I got in my car and drove back to the hotel.

I stopped and said hello to the girl at the front desk. I wondered if that made her a murder suspect. I figured that was stretching it a bit. I wondered if I was losing my marbles. I figured that wasn't quite so much of a stretch.

I went up to my room and lay down on the bed. Time to rest up for the main event. Fifteen rounds with the heavyweight champion, Murdering Minton. And me in the role of Rocky. I should have been in training. I should have been downstairs in the hotel kitchen, punching out slabs of beef. Except they didn't have slabs of beef in the hotel kitchen, they only had a sandwich shop. Well, fuck it, I didn't feel like jogging all the way back to Atlantic City, running up the front steps of Tallman's Casino, and jumping up and down with my arms in the air, either. No, I'd train for this one lying down.

I called my wife, told her things were going well and I'd probably be home in a couple of days. She seemed glad to hear it.

I didn't bother calling MacAullif. I knew he was

busy. After all, he had three murders on his hands and I only had two. I also wanted to wrap things up before I made my report.

I called Richard, though. He was glad to hear from me, too, what with me being a murder suspect and all.

"Minton get back from Vegas?" Richard asked.

"Sure did."

"Everything work out all right?"

"Like a charm."

"I knew it would," Richard said. "The cops let you go?"

"Of course."

"That's good," Richard said. "You have any more problems, you call me right away."

"First thing," I told him.

"You sure everything's all right now?" he asked.

"Just fine."

"That's real good," Richard said, "because Wendy found this photo assignment . . ."

I finally got off the phone, but not before I'd accepted an assignment to shoot a department store escalator that some stupid kid had managed to get his finger stuck in. I felt like refusing it: "Sorry, Wendy, I don't do this kind of shit anymore. I'm a full-fledged murder suspect." But I figured she wouldn't understand. I just meekly took down the info and told her I'd do it.

I hung up the phone and lay there, thinking, gee, while I was at it, was there anyone else I wanted to call?

Oh, yeah.

That's right.

Minton.

I called the Minton Agency. I recognized the dumb secretary's voice on the phone.

"Minton Agency," she said.

"This is Stanley Hastings. The murderer. I'd like to talk to Mr. Minton."

I heard a sharp intake of breath, followed by the most wonderful silence. I could almost see her mind racing, trying to figure out what to do. Finally she figured it out, because suddenly I was on hold. About thirty seconds later, Minton's voice came on the line.

"Mr. Hastings?"

"Yes. Mr. Minton. Did you get the money?"

"I have it. Now I'll tell you where to bring the pictures."

"Sorry, Minton, but we're playing in my ballpark. You don't tell me where to bring the pictures. I tell you where to bring the cash."

"I don't like that."

"That's too bad, because it's my ball, and if you don't want to play, I'm gonna take it and go home."

There was a silence, then, "All right. Where do you want?"

I gave him the address of the alley.

"What time?" Minton asked.

"How's nine o'clock tonight?"

"I'll be there."

I couldn't resist.

"Dress casual."

37

This was it. The big scene. The shootout at the O.K. Corral. High noon, if you can have high noon at nine o'clock at night. Mano a mano. Just me and the other gunslinger.

There was only one thing wrong, and that was the word "other." Other implies more than one. But there was only one gunslinger: Minton. I was, as usual, unarmed.

Can you have a shootout between two guys when one of them is unarmed? I know you can have a shooting. But can you have a shootout? I realized it was simply a matter of semantics. The problem was, it was also a matter of survival. You see, I was kind of counting on surviving the final scene. I know the tragic hero's supposed to die in it, but this wasn't Greek tragedy, this was real life.

And real life implies real death.

And there you are. And there I was. Being brave. But not as brave as I would have been if it weren't for the cops. I was banking on the cops. They were the cavalry, riding in to save the end of the scene. I guess the cavalry doesn't really arrive in *High Noon* or *Gunfight at the O.K. Corral,* but you know what I mean.

So while I might want to call this my big scene, I knew it wasn't really one on one.

I parked about a half a block away from the alley. It was a quarter to nine. I got out and looked up and down the street. There was no one in sight. The street light was half a block away. It was dark as all hell.

I straightened my tie and smoothed out my jacket. I straightened my gun-belt. I wasn't wearing a gun-belt, but I straightened it, which gives you some idea of where my head was at.

I walked out into the middle of the street. I walked down the middle of the street to the alley. There was no reason for walking in the middle of the street. It just seemed cinematic. I realized I was walking slightly bowlegged.

I unbuttoned my jacket, pushed it back from my hip. Ready for the fast draw.

I reached the mouth of the alley. It was dark as bloody fucking hell. As I'd anticipated, by night the doorways and alcoves were dark as pitch, and perfect for anyone to hide in.

I'd come early on purpose. I wanted to give the cops tailing me a chance to settle in.

I walked into the alley. Step by step.

I stopped half-way down. This was it. This was the place.

But now what? Shit. I should have had a signal. I should have told him I'd light a match. Or cough three times. Or something like that. I hadn't even thought of it. Because I'm an amateur and I don't know how to do these things. Well, if I don't get killed, I'll learn.

Waiting is a bitch. I don't know anyone who likes waiting. I mean, when they put out lists of leisure activities people enjoy, you never see "waiting" on any of them. Or you're talking to someone and they say, "Hey, I really like waiting, you know what I mean?" It just doesn't happen. Waiting for the dentist. Waiting for your kid at camp. Waiting for your wife—that's a biggie. Waiting for Christmas, when you were a kid. Waiting for Godot. Or Lefty. Yeah, no one really likes that.

But they all beat waiting for a murderer.

I caught a flash of movement in the alley up ahead on my right. Good. That would be the cops settling in. I wanted them in position before Minton showed, of course. That cop had managed to maneuver around by me in the dark. He'd be behind me. But there'd have to be another cop at the mouth of the alley, where Minton would come from. He'd be behind Minton. He was the one I was counting on. In fact, to be honest, I hoped there'd be more than just two.

The cop I had spotted moving, moved again. He stepped out from the shadows where he was hiding into the middle of the alley. I could see him better now—my eyes were growing accustomed to the dark. He moved again, and what little light there was filtering down from the street fell on his face.

It was Minton.

I shouldn't have been so surprised. After all, I'd asked Minton to be here, and here he was. True, he was a few minutes early, but then so was I. No, I shouldn't have been surprised. But the fact was, I almost jumped out of my shoes. It was like being in a funhouse when suddenly a face jumps out at you. A scary face. One you don't want to see.

The thing was, I didn't want to act scared. For one thing, it would ruin my image as a private detective. For another thing, it would probably get me killed. I didn't want to act scared, but I was. Jesus Christ! Well, if that's Minton, where's the cops? Where the hell's the fucking cops?

Minton stood there, feet slightly apart, weight nicely balanced, I was sure, ready for the quick draw.

I stood there with my heart in my mouth.

"Hastings?" Minton said.

I wasn't to be outdone. "Minton," I said back.

I think the next line should have been, "This town's not big enough for the two of us," but apparently Minton hadn't read the script. "You bring the pictures?" he said.

I was ready for that question. I figured there were only two answers, and if I picked the wrong one I'd wind up dead.

"No," I said.

Minton took a step forward, ominously.

"You were supposed to bring the pictures," he growled.

"I know that," I said. "But you see, I'm not as stupid as I look. You've already killed two people. I figure if I had the pictures on me, you just might go for three."

He took another step.

"Where's the pictures?" he growled.

"The pictures are in an envelope, waiting to be delivered to the police in the event I don't make it out of this alley."

"Yeah," Minton said. "Tallman called me. He said you used that line on him. It's an old gag."

"I know. That's what I told Tallman. The thing is, I'm not very inventive. I believe in the tried and true."

"Maybe. I think you're bluffing."

"Oh?"

"Tallman fell for that, but I don't. We've only got your word for it what's in those pictures. You say they're shots of Tallman and Nubar. Could be. But they could be shots of Steerwell's girlfriend, for all we know. I say you're bluffing. I say you got nothing."

"Then you say wrong. Steerwell had shots of Tallman and Nubar together. That's what you were afraid of. That's why he wanted in on your little deal. The deal with you and Tallman.

"You liked the idea of being Tallman's silent partner. You didn't need someone else horning in. So you rubbed Steerwell out. Just like you rubbed out Nubar."

"You're full of shit."

"Maybe. Maybe not."

"And you're unlucky."

"That I know."

"See, the way I figure it, even if there are shots of Tallman and Nubar and you send them to the cops, they prove nothing. It's even money the cops aren't even going to act on them."

"You figure wrong. You see, I enclosed a letter."

"A letter?"

"Yeah. A letter. To the cops. Wanna hear it? I can't remember it word for word—it's a long letter—but I can give you the gist. At least let me tell you how it starts. 'Major Crimes Division, Northfield, Attention Lieutenant Barnes: Since you are reading this, it means that I am dead. I was killed by Mr. Minton of the Minton Detective Agency. He killed me in an attempt to cover up his role in two other murders, that of Joseph T. Steerwell and that of Frederick Nubar.' It goes on for a couple of pages. It explains how you flew to Vegas and then had a private plane fly you back. It explains how Tallman was in so deep to Nubar that he cut a deal with you to get Nubar out of the way. So you set Nubar up to get killed. Then when Steerwell tried to horn in on the deal, you rubbed him out, too. It explains how you falsely identified me as the guy who hired Steerwell because the other witnesses had blown the identification, and how you, being guilty of the murders and wanting a fall guy, hopped on the bandwagon and identified me, too.

"It's a great letter. It's one of the best things I ever wrote. In fact, if I could write that well all the time, I'd make a living at it, and I wouldn't have to do this private detective shit."

Minton shrugged. "Maybe, but I still think you're bluffing." His hand flicked. "You know what this is?"

I knew what it was. That is, I didn't know the make or the caliber, but I knew it was an automatic pistol with a silencer.

I'd had a gun pulled on me once before, back when I first started working for Richard, by an irate husband who didn't take kindly to the idea of being served with a divorce complaint. While it scared me to death, at least that time I didn't figure the guy intended to use it.

I figured Minton did.

Remind me never to hire myself out as a prognosticator. As usual, I figured wrong.

"Relax," Minton said. "I'm not going to shoot you with it. I just wondered if you knew what it was. Obviously you don't. So I'll tell you. This is the gun that killed Nubar."

I wouldn't have thought my eyes could have gotten any wider, but they must have, because I could see Minton's grin.

"Means something to you, does it? Just beginning to get the picture, aren't you?"

"No," I said. "No, I don't understand at all."

I was fighting for time. Hoping he'd talk. Hoping he'd give the cops a chance to move in.

"No," I repeated. "I don't understand at all. You ditched the gun you used on Steerwell. I figured you'd ditch the gun you used on Nubar."

"You figured wrong. I ditched the gun at Steerwell's

because something happened. I'd just plugged him and a car drove up. Naturally I didn't want to get caught with the rod. I dropped it on the floor beside him and slipped out the back door. I crept around the house and saw the guy going in. It wasn't the cops or anything, it was only the punk who hired him. I figured, great, the perfect fall guy, let him find the gun. I figured he'd panic and take it with him. Then he'd be fucked. He didn't, and then some crazy broad picked it up, but that's all right. He got the credit for bringing it. So when he went in the house, I hopped in my car and took off.

"I had this other gun in the car. Same model. Absolutely cold. No way to make a trace, an essential in my profession. I took it, went out and plugged Nubar. But I didn't ditch this gun. I kept it for an occasion just like this."

He grinned at me. "Now *I'll* tell *you* what happened. You hired Steerwell, and you killed him, too. You also killed Nubar. You had it in for me because I identified you. I was the one who was going to put you away. You figured I was the main witness, without me the case would fall apart, so you decided to do me in, too. Now, I don't know about the pictures or any letter you wrote to the cops. I think it's bullshit. If you did, well, it's because you were trying to frame me for the murders.

"But here's what happened. You came to my office this afternoon and threatened me. My secretary can vouch for that. You admitted you had the pictures. You told me to meet you out here and you'd give them back.

"I didn't care about those pictures, but I wanted to know what your game was, so I came. When I got here you pulled a gun."

He shifted it into his left hand and held it on me.

"This gun. The gun you used to kill Nubar. You fired a shot at me with this gun and you missed.

"And that's when I shot you with this one."

Quick draw Minton. His hand flicked and suddenly there was something in it. A tough private eye would have said he saw a glint of blue steel. Frankly, I didn't see shit. But I knew damn well the son of a bitch was holding a gun.

Minton took another step in.

"I'll put the Nubar gun in your hand and fire off a shot. That will put your fingerprints on the gun and the powder marks on your hand, so the paraffin test will show you fired it. I don't like it much. I'll have to claim I shot you, and the whole bit. But it will be self-defense. And under the circumstances, it's the best I can do."

He moved in another step. He wanted to be so close he couldn't miss. There were only ten feet between us now. I figured a little closer and he'd fire.

What should I do? What *could* I do? I didn't know. I had no idea. "PRIVATE DETECTIVE HASN'T A CLUE: Stands Like Dope, Gets Shot in Face."

What thoughts run through your mind at a time like that? I know what thoughts ran through mine: "We Polked 'em in '44, and we'll Pierce 'em in '52." I don't know if that was an actual campaign slogan, or if our American History teacher just made it up, but that was the maxim my classmates and I used to learn the terms of office of two of the more obscure presidents, James K. Polk, elected in 1844, and Franklin Pierce, elected in 1852. "And Zachary Taylor up the middle" was the saying that got us 1848. That, obviously, was no slogan—I made that one up myself.

At any rate, that's what flashed through my mind: "We Polked 'em in '44, and we'll Pierce 'em in '52." I bet an analyst could get some mileage out of that.

Polk and Pierce are both prodding terms, obvious phallic symbolism. Plus the fact that I was about to be Polked and Pierced by a bullet, a bullet shot by a gun, another phallic extension. Yeah, a shrink would have a field day with that.

But I think the real explanation was much simpler than that. I think it was simple regression to childhood. Wanting to be a kid again. Wanting to have no cares or responsibilities. Harkening back to a time when your biggest problem was who was president when. Not how you gonna feed your wife and kids, are you gonna stay out of jail, and will you stop a bullet.

Yeah, that's what I think it was.

My own version of *Rosebud*.

Minton leveled the gun and I knew the time had come.

So this is it. It all ends here. Bang. Silence. Darkness. The Void. Never to see my kid grow up. Never to write the great American novel. To die unknown. Unpublished. Unsung.

Unpaid.

To die for nothing, literally.

Some favor.

There was nothing I could do. Dodge? Dodge a bullet? That's an old expression, one used to describe someone achieving an impossible feat. Escaping in spite of overwhelming odds. That was all I had to do.

Sorry.

Not up to it.

Not even up to trying.

Stand like a schmuck and die.

Oh, shit!

Great. His last words were, "Oh, shit!"

A shadow moved in the dark behind Minton.

The cavalry.

A cop.

I saw an arm go up with something in it and come down on Minton's head, hard. There was a sick, thunking sound, and Minton slumped forward onto the ground. The shadow moved again as the cop bent over Minton, presumably to remove his gun, though it was too dark for me to see. The cop straightened, turned. Light fell on his face, and I gawked. The cop was MacAullif. He looked at me, and shook his head.

"You're not getting any better at this, are you?"

38

"What the hell are you doing here?"

"Just a minute," MacAullif said. He was busily engaged in tying Minton's hands behind him with a short cord that he'd taken out of his jacket pocket. "You gotta learn something about procedure. You secure the perpetrator first, *then* you talk." He gave the cord a final tug. "There. That ought to do it. Though I don't think this one's coming around for some time, anyway."

"What'd you hit him with?"

"Butt of a gun." MacAullif got to his feet. ".38 Special, if you're keepin' score."

I stared at him. "What are you doing here?"

"Savin' your ass, it looks like."

"No, I mean—"

"I know what you mean. I just thought you might need a little help."

"I thought you had three murders pending."

"One of the joys of being a sergeant is being able to delegate authority. I'm sure my boy Daniels is doing a hell of a job."

"When'd you get here?"

"Yesterday. I picked you up at your hotel yesterday afternoon. I've been on your tail ever since."

"Why? Why tail me? Why didn't you just let me know you were here?"

MacAullif cocked his head on one side. "That might have been easier, now, mightn't it? But the thing is, we don't seem to tell each other everything, do we? And the fact is, you were holding out on me. And with you holding out on me, I wanted to know what the real story was, not just the version you chose to give me. See what I mean?"

"Yeah. Yeah," I said. I have a very slow reaction time, and the whole thing was just beginning to dawn on me. "You're saying you've been following me since yesterday afternoon?"

"That's right."

"Then that means . . ."

"What?"

"The cops weren't."

"I'm a cop."

"No. The other cops. The Atlantic City cops. The boys from Major Crimes."

"I don't know them. I'm from New York."

"Yes, but . . ."

"But what?"

"They weren't following me."

"No one's been following you but me."

"You sure?"

"Hey. I'm a cop. I can spot a tail. Aside from me, you've been clean."

I told you I'm a slow take. The fact is, I said it again, just to nail it down.

"Then . . . the cops . . . *weren't* . . . following me."

"No."

I blinked twice. "Jesus Christ!"

"What?"

"I could have been killed!"

MacAullif nodded. "That seems entirely likely."

I felt completely numb. "Good lord," I murmured. My knees felt wobbly. "Excuse me," I said, "but I'm going to sit down."

I did. I was sorry to plummet so in MacAullif's estimation, but there was no help for it.

MacAullif grinned. "Ah! The old post-lookin'-down-the-mouth-of-the-gun-barrel syndrome. Don't worry. Cops get it, too. Rookies and veterans. Maybe not quite so dramatically, but they do."

I remembered something. "Oh, shit," I said.

"What?"

I reached in my inside jacket pocket. "Here's a trick I learned from you," I told him. I tugged it out.

"What's that?"

"It's a pocket dictaphone. My wife gave it to me last Christmas. I'm supposed to be writing the great American novel with it."

"Any luck?"

"Naw, it inhibits me. I can't think of what to say. This is the first time I used it."

I was glad about the dictaphone. It gave me something to do and something to talk about. Something mindless. Something mechanical.

I switched it off, ran it back a bit.

"Let's see if it came out."

I stopped it. Put it on play.

MacAullif's voice came over loud and clear, saying, "Ah! The old post-lookin'-down-the-mouth-of-the-gun-barrel syndrome."

I clicked it off.

"Came out great," I said.

"Yeah, nice work," MacAullif said. "But you gotta run it back and knock off the end of it."

"Why? Just 'cause I come off like a chickenshit asshole?"

"Don't be stupid," MacAullif said. "I'm sure they

know that already. The thing is, I don't want them to know I was here."

"Why not?"

"You're bein' stupid again." MacAullif spoke slowly and evenly, as if addressing a child. "My name is MacAullif. Why am I down here? The boys from Major Crimes aren't stupid. I don't want them getting a lead to my daughter."

"Right," I said. "I'm sorry. I guess looking at a gun kind of scrambles my wits."

"You didn't have much to start with," MacAullif said. "Just run it back and erase it."

"O.K.," I said. "We're gonna have to be quiet when I do. The only way to erase is to record, and the mike picks up everything, regardless of what the volume's set at. So when I switch it on, we can't talk."

"Probably a blessing," MacAullif said.

I ran it back to just before MacAullif knocked Minton on the head.

"Leave in the sound of the blow," MacAullif said.

"Why?"

"You knocked him out, then you switched off the machine."

"You think the cops are gonna buy that?"

"No, but it's the best story you got. And they can't disprove it. You leave out the blow, and the whole thing sounds fishy as hell."

I left in the sound of the blow. I switched the recorder on. MacAullif and I stood in silence for a couple of minutes. I switched it off record and put it on play. Dead air. I'd gone far enough. I switched it off and hit rewind to send the tape back to the top of the reel.

"O.K.," MacAullif said. "Now, we're lucky the son of a bitch didn't mention Harold. If he had, we have to ditch the tape. The way things stand, it's fine." He looked at me. "So the son of a bitch I.D.'d you instead of Harold?"

"Yeah."

"That was stupid. But if he wasn't stupid, you wouldn't have caught him. All right. The way things stand, there's no reason Harold's name should come up. It's peripheral and it's not important. If Minton mentions him, well, there's nothing we can do about that, but there's no reason why he should, and even if he does, the cops aren't gonna pay that much attention. We got Minton dead to rights. So the only problem we got is the felony rap they got on you for grabbing those pix."

"No problem. I can handle that."

"You sure?"

"Yeah, I'm sure. I'm handing them a murderer. They're gonna let the pix slide. Particularly if I give 'em the pictures back."

"Most of the pictures," MacAullif said.

"Absolutely."

"O.K.," MacAullif said. "You gotta call the cops, and I gotta get out of here. Now tell me, where do Harold and Barbara stand?"

"At the moment they stand nowhere, but they're gonna get their best shot. They've both had the shit scared out of them. They're gonna need help, and they're gonna find they got no one to cling to but each other."

"How do you know that?" MacAullif said.

"Well, Harold's little playmate's on her way home to Salt Lake City under an assumed name. The cops won't find her and Harold won't find her. She's out of it."

"And Barbara's friend?"

"Barbara's friend is out of it, too. He just doesn't know it yet."

"O.K.," MacAullif said. "Now I gotta go. There's a

pay phone on the corner. I'll watch this bird just to make sure he doesn't come to while you call the cops. As soon as you come back I'll take off."

"Fine."

"And listen," MacAullif said. "Hey. Thanks a lot."

"Don't mention it," I told him.

"Can you handle everything?" MacAullif said. "Is there anything you need?"

I thought a moment. "Yeah. Yeah, there is."

"What?"

"The gun you bopped Minton with. Is that your police issue?"

"Shit, no," MacAullif said. "On a job like this I carry my own piece."

"Fine," I said. "Look. I'm staying at the Comfort Inn on Route 30. On your way out of town just put it in a box with my name on it and leave it at the desk."

MacAullif looked at me. "You serious?"

"Absolutely," I told him.

"O.K.," he said. "Anything else?"

"Yeah," I said.

"What's that?"

"Take the bullets out of it, would you? I don't wanna shoot myself in the leg."

39

I was fulfilling a life-long fantasy. It was something I'd always dreamed of doing. It was something I'd been reading about in detective stories all my life. The hero captures the bad guy single-handed, ties him hand and foot, and calls the cops to come pick him up.

Of course, I hadn't really captured Minton single-handed, but the cops didn't know that. They suspected it, but they didn't know it.

Barnes switched the recorder off and cocked his head at me.

"The end of this recording's been erased," he said.

"Oh, really?" I said.

"Yeah, really. The mike is on, but there's nothing happening. The recording has been recorded over. It's been erased. It's just dead air."

"Of course, it's dead air," I said. "After I hit Minton, who was I gonna talk to?"

Barnes shook his head. "No, no, no. It's been erased. You can tell the difference. There's a click. The click of the recorder being switched on when you recorded over the end."

"Or maybe that's the click of me shutting it off," I said.

"And then what's the recording beyond there?"

"Oh, something I recorded at another time," I said. "Perhaps when I was working on a book. That's what my wife gave me this thing for, you see. To write books."

"Is it your usual practice to record long passages of dead air?" Barnes asked.

"Well, my thought process is sometimes a little slow."

"You can say that again."

We were standing near the mouth of the alley. Preston came out along with two officers leading the handcuffed Minton. They stuck him in the back of a patrol car. The cops got in and drove off. Preston walked up to us.

"Clam got anything to say?" Preston asked.

"He not only says it, he taped it," Barnes said. "You can have a listen yourself when we get back."

"Any good?" Preston asked.

"Not bad. It fries Minton's ass."

"I'm sure it does. So the clam came through, huh?"

"Well, I'm sure he had help," Barnes said. "The thing is, he erased the end of the tape recording, so we'll never know. So I guess we have to credit him with the collar."

"I suppose so. Though you know and I know this guy would have trouble bringing back a runaway three-year-old."

"May I say something?" I said.

"Boy, the clam's talkative," Preston said.

"It's the thrill of the capture," Barnes said. "Does it every time."

"What do you want to say, clam?"

I looked at them accusingly. "You guys weren't following me."

"What?"

"When you let me go the second time. You didn't have me followed."

"Of course not. Why?"

"You almost got me killed."

"What?"

"I was counting on you guys following me. I figured you'd be there, backing me up. See, I couldn't think of any reason why you would have let me go unless you were gonna have me followed."

Barnes and Preston looked at each other and shook their heads.

"That's because you have such an exaggerated sense of your own importance," Barnes said. "And, if I may say so, because you have such a low opinion of police intelligence. You want me to tell you why we let you go? We let you go because you were innocent. Bizarre concept? You were innocent. You're a meddling, interfering private eye, but you didn't kill those guys. I knew it. Preston knew it. But you didn't give us credit for that, see. You think you're the only one with any smarts. Why don't you tell him how it was, Preston?"

Preston shrugged. "Sure. As soon as Minton I.D.'d you as the guy who hired Steerwell, we knew he was the perp. Just like you did. See, the way we figured it, there was no way you and your estimable asshole attorney could be so stupid as to claim that Minton would confirm your story if you knew, in fact, that he would not. So, when he failed to confirm your story, we knew he was lying and knew he was guilty. It was an incredibly stupid thing for Minton to do by the way. In fact, all of the principals in this affair were incredibly stupid. They had to be. Otherwise, you would never have figured it out."

Just what MacAullif had said. Any more and I might begin to believe it.

"But leave that," Preston went on. "The fact is, we knew Minton was guilty. So why should we bother about you? We put in the past few days working on him. We dug into his background, and it's amazing what we've established. We can link him to Tallman. We can link him to Nubar. We also got a line on the pilot who flew him back from Vegas, and when we get ahold of him I'm sure he's gonna sing."

"So, you see," Barnes said, "in another twenty-four hours we'd have cracked this case ourselves."

"Not that we don't appreciate the help," Preston said. "Though it would have been better if you'd let Minton shoot you. His murder of you would have been the ultimate admission of guilt."

"But you did help in your own way," Barnes said, "and we will certainly give you credit in the press."

"Thanks, but no thanks," I told him. "I'm sort of a low-profile type myself, and the less need said about me, the better."

"Suit yourself," Barnes said, "but if that's the way you want to play it, the fact is we probably won't need you at all. Or your tape recording. We'll pick up Tallman tonight, shake him down, get these guys ratting on each other. That should do it right there."

"I'm glad to hear it," I said.

"But there is one small matter," Barnes said.

"Oh?"

"The pictures."

"Ah, yes, the pictures," I said.

"Yes," Preston said. "We were wondering if those pictures might form some important link in this case."

"I don't know. They certainly might," I said.

"And there is that felony count of grand larceny," Barnes said.

"There is indeed," I said. "Well, gentlemen, I was just wondering. If I were to, quote, find those pictures, unquote, and drop 'em by Major Crimes tomorrow morning, do you suppose that felony count might just disappear?"

"It's entirely likely," Barnes said. "In fact, I'm sure the whole thing could be dismissed in absentia, without the defendant ever having to come back and appear in court."

"That would be right nice," I told him. "Now look, if you boys have everything all wrapped up here, personally I've had a hell of a day and I'd like to get some sleep."

"No problem," Barnes said. "But—"

"What?"

"See you tomorrow?"

"First thing in the morning," I told him.

"Fine," Barnes said.

I turned to go.

"Just one thing," Barnes called after me.

I turned back. "What?"

"It's none of my business," Barnes said. "But if you wouldn't mind a little constructive criticism."

What could I say? Who *doesn't* mind a little constructive criticism?

"What's that?" I asked.

Barnes shrugged. "I think you probably read too much detective fiction."

40

I didn't stop by Major Crimes first thing the next morning. I had some other business to take care of first. Eight o'clock in the morning I was stationed in front of Johnson's Tree Surgeons when the young stud with the curly blond hair drove up in a beat-up Ford, unlocked the door, and hopped into one of the trucks. He gunned the motor and drove out. I tagged along behind.

He drove about four blocks, stopped for coffee and doughnuts to go and then headed out of town.

From about a half a block back, I could see him munching the doughnuts as he drove along. I wished I had some myself, but I'd skipped coffee and doughnuts that morning, having learned my lesson about drinking coffee on stakeout with no available bathroom in sight.

The guy drove about five miles out in the country and stopped under—guess what?—a tree. The tree looked healthy enough to me, but it was probably infested with something or other and was about to lose some of its limbs.

Well, the ace private detective to the rescue. Here I come to save a tree.

I parked my car about a half a block behind so he

wouldn't see it, got out and walked down the street. I found out there wasn't any particular need for me to rush to save this particular tree, 'cause when I got there the guy had not yet begun to unload his chainsaws, ropes or what-have-you. Instead he was sitting on the running board of the truck, finishing the coffee and doughnuts.

I strode up to him, stopped and in my best tough-guy manner, talking out of the side of my mouth, said, "Stand up."

He looked at me. "What?"

"I said, stand up. I want to talk to you."

He put down the cup of coffee and stood, muscles rippling. He was my height and weight, only really in shape, and I suddenly realized this guy could easily tear me apart. I couldn't let it phase me though. I stood my ground.

"Who the hell are you?" he demanded.

"My name is Harold Dunleavy," I said. "That mean anything to you?"

It did. His eyes flicked.

I had no way of knowing if this guy knew who Harold Dunleavy was and knew I wasn't him, but it didn't really matter. He could think I was Harold Dunleavy, or he could think I was some guy sent by Harold Dunleavy. Either way was just fine.

The kid cocked his head. "Oh, yeah?" he said, arrogantly.

The kid wasn't happy to see me, but he'd come to the realization that he could take me, and now he was actually gonna have some fun lording it over me for having taken my wife.

"Now, there's no reason for you and me to be at odds," I told him. "I just thought you and I should have a little talk."

"Yeah? And why is that?"

"It's my job," I told him.

That stopped him. He hadn't expected that line at all.

"What?"

"Yeah. Because of my job. You know what I do? Well, let me tell you. I'm a stockbroker. But you see, a stockbroker's salary ain't for shit. Just like a tree surgeon's. There's never enough money to go around, you know what I mean?"

I'd hit a chord anyone would respond to.

"Damn right," he said.

"Yeah," I said. "So that's why I do this other job. And that's the one I want to talk to you about."

"Oh?" he said, suspicious again.

"Yeah," I said. "I don't normally talk about it, but in your case I make an exception. You see how it is, this is a gambling town. I happen to have connections. You know what it means to have connections?"

"No."

"Well, I'll tell you. I'm connected to some people. Big people. And sometimes I do a job for 'em, you understand? I'm an independent contractor. I do contract work. You know what that means, contract work?"

"No."

"Good. I don't want you to. But here's the thing. The guys I'm working with. The guys I'm connected with. They judge me. They always judge me. See, because I'm supposed to be tough. That's part of my job, you know. Being tough."

The guy was looking at me as if I were from another planet. It was clear that he had no idea what I was talking about. It was also clear that he was slightly afraid that he was going to find out.

"The thing is," I said, "I can't afford to appear foolish."

He was staring at me now. "What?"

"Yeah. Foolish. And there's nothing that makes a guy look quite so foolish as to have some punk kid screwing his wife."

"Oh, yeah," he said again, but it wasn't quite as arrogant as when he said it before.

"Yeah," I said. "See, if the word got around to the guys that I deal with, they would think it made me look foolish. And then the next time a contract came along, they'd think twice before they gave it to me. See what I mean?"

"No. I don't see what you mean. What are you talking about, contract?"

I laughed. "You're dumber than you look. Either you know what I'm talking about, or you don't. If you don't, I don't particularly care. You ever see the film *Prizzi's Honor*?"

He gulped. "Yeah. I saw it."

"Good. Funny movie," I said. "Now, here's the thing."

I gave him my best tough-guy leer. I reached under my jacket and pulled the gun out of my belt. Fortunately, MacAullif had taken the bullets out of it as I'd requested, so I didn't blow my dick off, which might have damaged my tough-guy image some.

His eyes were round as saucers. I didn't aim the gun at him. I just held it and patted it softly a couple of times into my other hand.

I smiled at him and said it quite casually.

"If you ever come near my wife again, I'll blow your fucking head off."

41

"**T**here's twelve rolls of film here."

Barnes was right. I'd burned the thirteenth roll just as soon as I'd picked them up at the post office. I'd burned the roll with the pictures of MacAullif's daughter on it, just as I should have done to begin with.

It wasn't easy to do. I didn't want to go back to the hotel, because I was afraid Barnes might have sent a reception committee for me, seeing as how I was late getting to Major Crimes, what with having to deal with the tree surgeon and all. So I drove around till I found a roadside rest area, and I burned them one at a time with a book of matches into a garbage drum. I was paranoid as all hell that some cop would drive by and see me doing it, but none did. But I sure confused the hell out of a family of tourists having an early picnic lunch.

I looked at Barnes. "That's right," I said. "Twelve rolls."

"The girl from the Photomat said there were thirteen."

"Yeah," I said, "but she also claims I'm the guy who picked them up to begin with. And if she's as unreliable a witness as all that, she's probably wrong about the number, too."

"The guy does have a sense of humor," Preston said.

"He does, indeed," Barnes said. "The guy likes funny things. And you know, it's a funny thing about these pictures."

"What's that?" I said.

"Well, our theory," Barnes said, "Preston's and mine, has always been that you had some client that you were protecting and that's why you were a clam. And wouldn't it be a funny thing if that client that you were protecting happened to be on that thirteenth roll of film that Steerwell shot?"

"Highly funny," I said. "And also highly unlikely, wouldn't you say?"

"No, I wouldn't say," Barnes said. "But I would say this. You're very lucky. Don't you think so, Preston?"

"Yeah," Preston said. "I would say that he is very lucky."

"Very lucky. You're very lucky in that we don't give a shit. Seeing as how the pictures on the twelve rolls that you *did* give us—the pictures of Tallman and Nubar—happen to be exactly what we want, the number of rolls doesn't really matter that much.

"And the other thing is that the case is all wrapped up."

"Oh?"

"Yeah," Barnes said. "We rousted Tallman out of bed at three in the morning, gave him the works and he caved in just like that. He admits his connection with Nubar. He admits his connection with Minton. Claims he knew nothing about the murders—it was a shock to him. Blames it all on Minton."

"On the other hand," Preston said, "Minton's a clam. Just like you. Minton ain't saying a word."

"Oh?"

"Yeah. Minton denied everything, then clammed

and called a lawyer. Minton's not talking, but the lawyer's talking plenty. Claims it's all a frame-up. Claims Tallman's the actual perp and is trying to put it all off on Minton. Claims Tallman was the guy who was involved with Nubar. Tallman was the guy who had everything to lose. Claims if Steerwell took pictures of Tallman, then Steerwell was a threat to Tallman, not to Minton. If Minton was in that alley, he was there as a reputable private detective investigating a murder, and the person that he was meeting was probably a hit man sent by Tallman. And that hit man was the man who had the murder gun. Minton was there in his official capacity, attempting to recover pictures which were the rightful property of his agency. In other words, Minton is squeaky clean and being framed."

Barnes shrugged. "The guy had a lot of points."

"So what did you do?" I said.

"Hell," Preston said. "We just let the guy talk. We don't give a shit."

"Yeah," Barnes said. "In a couple of days, when things have cooled down, we'll get this attorney in here and we'll play him your tape recording. Then we'll explain to him how things are. Then, after we've shown him that we have Minton's balls in a vise, we will offer to let him make a deal. The deal, of course, is to cop a plea and turn state's evidence against Tallman."

"But don't think that means Minton's gonna walk," Preston said. "The best deal this guy's gonna cut, the way things stand, is the difference between twenty-five to life and ten to twenty-five."

"That's the best he's gonna get," Barnes said. "And that's only if we nail Tallman for the identical rap. And you see, if that happens—and I can almost assure you it will—we're not gonna need you or your recording at all."

"So you're lucky," Preston said. "You're lucky all the way up and down the line."

"That's right," Barnes said. "Particularly seeing as how we had such a good case against you for the murder, if we really wanted to press it. I mean, we had all that eyewitness identification, plus we found out a cop nailed you for speeding on Ventnor Avenue. The citation indicates you were hot-footing it away from Steerwell's just as fast as you could go not ten minutes after the time the witness says you ran in and out of the house."

"Yeah," Preston said. "Put that all together and throw in your fingerprints on Nubar's wallet, and see how lucky you are to be out here walking around."

"Yeah," Barnes said. "If you want to believe all that detective fiction, it's a wonder some dumb cop didn't look any further than you for the murder suspect."

I couldn't really think of anything to say, so I didn't.

"Now," Barnes said, "it's certainly been fun having you around here, but I'm just wondering when your business for this Mr. Richard Rosenberg might be finished and you might be heading back for New York."

"I was thinking of checking out tomorrow morning."

"We'll be sorry to see you go," Preston said.

"Oh?"

"Yeah. I don't think we'll have any problem handling Major Crimes and all that, but this certainly was an amusing break from our usual routine."

I looked from one to the other. I felt, as usual, pretty stupid. "That's nice to hear," I said. "I don't suppose you boys fix speeding tickets?"

"Certainly not," Barnes said. "We're not corrupt."

"I'm certainly glad to hear it," I said. "Well boys,

it's been nice talking to you, but I guess I'll be shoving off now."

"You staying one more night?" Barnes said.

"That's right," I told him.

"Well then, you mind if I give you a little advice?"

Jesus. Again with the advice.

"Would it matter if I did?" I said.

"Just trying to be helpful," Barnes said.

I shrugged. "Yeah, sure. What's your advice?"

"Well," Barnes said. "If I were you, I wouldn't gamble."

Strange advice in Atlantic City. I looked at him. "Oh?"

"Yeah." Barnes looked at Preston and then grinned at me. "I would say you've probably used up your allotment of luck."

42

I felt like the fucking Lone Ranger.

Harold and Barbara were sitting on their living room couch. I was standing in front of them.

I'd rung the front doorbell, and when Harold had come to the door, I'd said brusquely, "It's about the murders," and pushed by him into the house. He'd followed me into the living room in a daze, at which point I'd curtly ordered him to get his wife. I don't know if they can nail you for impersonating an officer just by being rude, but it occurred to me at the time it would be interesting to hear someone argue the point. At any rate, it sure as hell worked, and there they were, America's favorite fun couple, sitting on the couch, gaping up at me as if I were the whole fucking FBI.

"Now," I said, "I'd like to relieve your minds. You're not charged with anything, and you're not gonna be. We're winding up these murder cases now, and we need to clear the air. Now I have to tell you some things. Some of it's gonna be news to one of you, some it's gonna be news to the other. Some of it will be stuff one of you knows, some of it will be stuff the other of you knows, and some of it will be stuff neither of you heard before. It doesn't matter. Just sit there and listen, don't interrupt, and let me get through it. You're gonna hear it all, but what I wanna impress upon you is, nothing I say goes any further than this room. Is that understood?"

They nodded at me.

"All right. Here's the scene. Tallman, the owner of Tallman's Casino, and Minton, the owner of Minton's Detective Agency, are going to jail for murder. The murder of Frederick Nubar and the murder of Joseph T. Steerwell."

There was stirring on the couch. Both Harold and Barbara were ready to speak.

"Shut up," I said. "I told you, I don't want you to interrupt. I'm going to tell it all.

"Now, we've been on to Tallman for some time. This goes back to a few months ago when we approached Harold Dunleavy and asked him to do a job for us."

Barbara Dunleavy stared at me. Her eyes were wide. She turned and looked at her husband. Harold Dunleavy's eyes were wide, too, and his jaw was actually open. He was gaping at me, but, thanks to my several admonitions, he wasn't about to interrupt.

"You see, Mrs. Dunleavy," I went on, "seeing as how Harold was both a stockbroker and a gambler, it made him the perfect person to get close to Tallman. So we approached him with a proposition. I say we— Harold's never met me before—but my men approached him. And I must confess, at our insistence, he was not allowed to say anything to you."

Barbara looked at Harold. Harold looked at Barbara. I don't know how to describe those looks, except to say they were pretty phenomenal.

I didn't want the two of them looking at each other, so I went on hurriedly.

"That's how it was," I said. "Now it happened that

Tallman had a girlfriend. A blackjack dealer in the casino. We figured she was the best way to get a line on Tallman, so we asked Harold to cultivate her. Now I have to apologize for this, Mrs. Dunleavy, 'cause I'm sure it was very hard on you, particularly with Harold instructed not to tell you anything. But that's the way it had to be.

"Anyway, through her, Harold got a line on Tallman. And what he found out was Tallman was connected to a loan shark named Frederick Nubar. That's how Tallman got all his financing for the casino. It was a secret. It was something that, if it got out, would have wrecked Tallman's empire. It was hot news. Only two other people knew this. Minton, who was shaking down Tallman, and Steerwell, who was attempting to do the same thing.

"Steerwell was the added starter. We already knew about Tallman and Minton, but it was late in the game when we tipped to Steerwell. And that's because it was late in the game when Steerwell tipped to the play.

"Of course, when we found out about it we asked Harold to get a line on Steerwell. He was a natural for the job. Of course, no one knew he was working for us. And he was the guy with the ins all around. He was perfect.

"Which brings us to the day of the murders.

"Now, I'll tell you briefly what actually happened, 'cause neither of you know. Minton and Tallman decided to kill Nubar. Tallman was deep in hock to him and saw no other way to get out. He didn't have the guts to do it himself, so he offered Minton a partnership for doing the job. They decided to kill Steerwell at the same time because he was trying to muscle in on their racket.

"Here's what happened. The day before the crime,

Minton flew to Vegas, presumably on business. Then he had a private plane fly him back.

"That's where the comedy begins, and that's how we got in this mess."

I stopped and looked at them. They were staring at me, wide eyed. I was ready to plunge ahead, to make sure neither one of them interrupted and said a word. I realized it wasn't necessary. At that moment I don't think either one of them would have been capable of speech.

"So here's what happened. Minton drove out to Steerwell's. Steerwell wasn't surprised to see him. He hadn't known Minton had supposedly gone to Vegas, 'cause Minton hadn't told him. And Minton was Steerwell's boss. So Steerwell invited him in, and Minton promptly pulled out a gun and shot him in the face.

"That's when the comedy begins. Harold, here, following our instructions, drove up to see Steerwell. Minton heard the car pull up and didn't want to get caught with the gun, so he dropped it on the floor and beat it out the back door. Harold came in, found Steerwell dead, didn't know what to do, and beat it out of there fast."

I turned to Barbara. "And that's where you come in, Mrs. Dunleavy."

I turned back to Harold. "See, Harold, the strain on your wife had been too much. Our fault, of course, but you can see how it would be. She was suspicious. Very suspicious. Particularly with you instructed not to say anything. So she followed you that day."

Harold started.

Barbara started.

But neither said a word.

"Yeah," I said. "That's what happened. She arranged for the kid to go home with a friend from school, and she got in the car, and she followed you. You can't blame her for that. You'd certainly given her enough reason. But that's what happened. She followed you to Steerwell's. And she saw you go in. And she saw you run out. She didn't know what had happened, but she sure as hell was determined to find out. As soon as you drove off, she pulled up, parked the car and went up to the house.

"The front door was unlocked. She pushed it open and went in. Of course, you know what she found. Steerwell's body was lying there on the floor. A gun with a silencer was lying there next to it.

"And that, Mr. Dunleavy, is when your wife did a dumb, heroic thing. You can't blame her for it, and neither can we, but I must say it did screw up the investigation for some time. Fortunately everything's straightened out now.

"Your wife saw the body and the gun lying there on the floor. And she jumped to a conclusion. She knew you were into something, and she didn't know how deep, but she thought this had confirmed it.

"She thought you'd killed Steerwell."

I paused and let that sink in.

"And that's when she did the thing that is both dumb and heroic. You may have given your wife a hard time, Mr. Dunleavy, and she may have given you a hard time, and life lately may not have been what you could refer to as marital bliss. But, underneath all that, your wife must still care for you a whole lot, because she took a terrible risk.

"She thought it was your gun, and she wanted to get rid of it. She picked it up and carried it out of the house. Unfortunately, at that moment, the next-door neighbor came out of her house and saw her. Your wife screamed, panicked, dropped the gun, hopped into her car and sped off."

FAVOR

Barbara MacAullif Dunleavy was now gawking at me with an expression identical to the one worn by Harold when I'd been talking about him.

"Now," I said, "naturally she's been in an absolute panic ever since. And you, Harold, you've been in an absolute panic ever since. And neither one of you've felt you were able to talk to the other. It must have been living hell for you.

"But the thing is, I'm here to tell you it's over. Harold, you've done a good job, but we don't need you anymore. We don't even need you to testify. We nailed these birds, and we got 'em dead to rights. As far as we're concerned, your job is over.

"And you, Mrs. Dunleavy, as far as we're concerned, you've done nothing wrong. Technically, you're guilty of failing to report a crime. Technically, so is Harold. But we're willing to overlook that. Particularly, under the circumstances. It only seems fair.

"So Harold, thanks for a job well done, and Mrs. Dunleavy, we're sorry to have inconvenienced you, we hope there's no hard feelings."

Harold and Barbara gawked at me. Then at each other. Then back at me.

All right, so it wasn't brilliant. I told you I'm not that good a writer. It was the best I could do. It was a story with more holes in it than a Swiss cheese. He knew everything I said about him was bullshit. And she knew everything I said about her was bullshit. And they probably both could assume what I was saying about the other one was bullshit, too.

But I figured it didn't matter. They could pretend to buy it and ride along. Or they could buy parts of it and discount other parts of it. Or they could admit the whole thing was bullshit. Frankly, I didn't care. The thing was, whatever they chose to do, they'd have to talk to each other.

And that was the best I could hope for.

But the talking would come later. For the moment they were speechless.

I smiled, bowed and started out.

It was Barbara who recovered first. I was halfway to the door before she stopped me.

"Who *are* you?" she said.

I turned and looked at her for one last time. Barbara MacAullif Dunleavy. Daughter of Sergeant MacAullif. The woman I'd admired from afar. She had risen and come to the door. And there she was. Up close at last.

The cheeks were every bit as smooth as they'd seemed. The face so young, so bright.

Barbara MacAullif Dunleavy. The woman I'd seen in dirty photographs with a young stud. The woman I'd thought deserved better. The woman I'd secretly thought deserved me.

Barbara MacAullif Dunleavy. The woman I'd done everything in my power to get back together again with her weak, philandering husband.

I looked at her that one last time.

I smiled slightly and, I'm sure, somewhat regretfully and then tossed the line away.

"Who *was* that masked man?" I said.

Then I was gone.

43

I laid the gun on MacAullif's desk.

"Thanks for the loan," I said.

MacAullif picked it up and slid it into a desk drawer.

"Don't mention it," he said. "Everything go all right?"

"Like clockwork. Minton and Tallman are going down."

"Fuck them," MacAullif said. "I mean the pictures."

"No problem. Twelve of thirteen rolls were duly delivered to the boys at Major Crimes, who were duly grateful."

"And Barbara's outside interest?"

"He's history."

"And Harold and Barbara?"

"They're getting their best shot. Whether they take it or not is up to them."

MacAullif nodded. "Best you could do." He looked at me. "Sorry you couldn't meet Barbara. She's quite a girl, you know."

"I'm sure she is," I told him. Holding out on MacAullif was getting to be a hard habit to break.

MacAullif looked embarrassed. I knew why. He wanted to say something that was awkward for him.

"I just want you to know—" he began.

"Skip it," I said.

"Right," he said. "Fuck it. But if there's ever anything I can do for you."

"I don't suppose you can fix Jersey traffic tickets?"

"Little out of my jurisdiction."

"That's what I figured. So how's your three murders going?"

"One lapsed and went in the 'Unsolved Crimes' file, one I'm working on and one Daniels actually solved."

"Not a bad batting average," I observed.

"Par for the course," MacAullif said.

I left him to grapple with the third murder. I was thankful it had nothing to do with me.

I wouldn't want you to think I'm entirely forgetful. On the way out, I checked his name on the certificates. The man I'd done the favor for was named William. Sergeant William MacAullif. I counted that as a particularly useless piece of information. I couldn't imagine myself ever calling MacAullif "Bill" or "Billy."

I got in the car and drove home. Alice and Tommie were glad to see me, absence making the heart grow fonder, and all that shit.

"How'd it go?" Alice asked.

"Not bad," I told her.

"Are they going to get back together again?"

"That's up to them. I did all I could."

"I'm sure you did. And I'm sure they will."

And she was sure, too. Alice has absolute confidence in my ability to do things. I wish I shared it.

Yeah, Alice was real pleased with the way things had turned out. Of course, I'd left out a few details in my account of what happened. Like the bit about almost getting nailed for two murders and one grand larceny charge. Little things like that.

So Alice probably didn't understand my reaction

later that evening, when she called out, "Honey?" as she has a habit of doing when she wants me to do some small thing for her, like pass her the *TV Guide* or get a roll of toilet paper or bring her a bowl of chocolate ice cream on my way back from the kitchen.

"Honey?" she called. "Do me a favor."

"No way."

About the Author

PARNELL HALL's first novel, *Detective,* was an Edgar Award nominee for Best New Mystery. His second novel, *Murder,* continued the antics and amateur sleuthing of Stanley Hastings. (Both are available in Onyx editions.) *Favor* is Hall's third Stanley Hastings mystery. Like his hero, Hall makes his home in New York City.